"I think this guy is
Carl Lyons whisp

"No, that's impossible," she said.

"I'd bet on it," Lyons answered, taking a closer look at the man, who was now less than twenty feet away from them. Something about his features seemed disturbingly familiar, and finally Lyons placed him. "He was in a file of mug shots of Cartel people we looked through at the Farm."

"You're sure?" she asked.

Lyons nodded, all the while keeping his eyes on Octria's rifle.

"That's too bad," Tyne said as she whipped her club around, catching Lyons squarely in the back of the head. The Ironman twisted in place from the force of the blow, reflexively battling to maintain his balance. It was a battle he quickly lost, and as a supernova of stars exploded inside his skull, Lyons felt himself falling....

Mack Bolan's

ABLE TEAM®
White Fire

Dick Stivers

A GOLD EAGLE BOOK FROM
WORLDWIDE®

TORONTO • NEW YORK • LONDON • PARIS
AMSTERDAM • STOCKHOLM • HAMBURG
ATHENS • MILAN • TOKYO • SYDNEY

First edition April 1989

ISBN 0-373-61241-9

Special thanks and acknowledgment to
Ron Renauld for his contribution to this work.

Printed in U.S.A.

1

Clark Meisner snapped a gnat from his bronzed forearm and uncapped his canteen as he stared at the verdant jungle before him. Thick with rampant growth and unmarked by any preexisting trail, it seemed even more impregnable than the land he and his expedition party had already spent the past day and a half hacking through. Aware of the human intrusion, macaws and monkeys in the treetops overhead raised a caterwaul, and Meisner felt as if he were being mocked for thinking he could traverse this land, much less explore it with any degree of efficiency.

As if she could read Meisner's thoughts, Tyne Murray moved closer to him and whispered, "Times like this, a boring office job back in the States doesn't seem quite so bad, does it?"

"I wouldn't go quite that far," Meisner smirked. "At least not yet. Another couple of days of this, though, and..."

"Let's not kid ourselves. We both love it here."

Meisner wiped sweat from his receding hairline and took a short sip from the canteen before passing it to Tyne. "I'll love it more once we find our first *Bos sauveli ornatus*."

He was referring to the spectacled kouprey, an exotic breed of wild ox whose nearest kin, the plain kouprey, had long topped the list of endangered species after being hunted to the verge of extinction in the forests of Cambodia. The kouprey was a distinctive beast, not only by virtue of its dwindling numbers, but also because of its breeding potential. When mated with the domesticated East Indian zebu, the hybrid offspring of the plain kouprey had the potential to revitalize strains of domestic cattle throughout all of Southeast Asia, which in turn could play a key role in battling the widespread hunger felt in that region of the globe. Scientists had long speculated that the spectacled strain of the ox was of a significantly heartier stock, but regrettably the animal had been hunted to such an extent that it had been written off as extinct for the past half century.

A year ago, however, Meisner had been browsing through a seven-year-old issue of *Nature Photographique* magazine when he'd come across a pictorial essay on the wilds of remote Caribbean Islands. Several of the photographs depicted the jungle interior of Skyler's Island, a speck of land roughly halfway between Brazil's northeast coast and the lower Antilles. Meisner had been astounded to see pictures of native Yanonli herdsmen tending small groups of cattle, which included several wild oxen with the telltale markings of *Bos sauveli ornatus* around their eyes. As a recently retired explorer and present board member of Miami's renowned Metrozoo, Meisner had become obsessed with the possibility that these supposedly extinct beasts had somehow managed to survive in such a totally unexpected habitat. Meticulously checking through old shipping records and all other available sources of information that he could get his hands on, Meisner succeeded in establishing a feasible explanation by which the koupreys could have been introduced to Skyler's Island back around the turn of the century.

Unfortunately, aside from the magazine article he could find no other mention of the oxen on that island over the previous twenty-two years, and the cameraman who had taken the photos of the Yanonli herdsmen had died soon after the article appeared. There was also no way of locating the names of anyone else associated with his expedition. Even more discouraging was the fact that during the intervening years the government of Skyler's Island had changed hands. The new regime was opposed to cooperating with Meisner and his proposal to venture back through the jungle to the lair of the Yanonli tribesmen in hopes of rediscovering the rare kouprey. His dream was to transport a number of the oxen back to Metrozoo for a carefully monitored breeding program, with the long-term goal of reintroducing the animals to their native Asian habitat.

Just when Meisner had been about to give up on the undertaking, his luck had changed through a chance meeting with Tyne Murray. Tyne was a recently retired CIA agent now working on Skyler's Island as adviser to a U.S.-based consortium, Coastal Sands Inc., which was currently involved in the development of a six-mile stretch of the isle's scenic southern beachfront. She'd heard of his plight through an acquaintance and, expressing a mutual intrigue with the mystery of the elusive kouprey, she'd helped grease the necessary skids for approval of his expedition. She had even arranged for partial financing of its costs, with the understanding that she'd accompany Meisner and that her backers would receive a share of the recognition and any potential rewards that might evolve from achieving the distinction of discovering a species thought to be extinct.

"I'm glad you haven't tried to renegotiate for a money-back guarantee on this trip," Meisner told the woman as he clipped the canteen back to his belt. "I mean, we've already covered more than twice the ground we planned on and we haven't even spotted a single Yanonli much less a kouprey."

"Well, the prime minister did say that after last year's floods there'd been a shift of tribal boundaries." Tyne dabbed at her brow with a bandanna already wet with perspiration. "With all this new growth there's hardly been a clearing large enough for grazing. But somewhere I'm sure we'll find one. Chin up. It's always darkest before the dawn, right?"

"If only they didn't have regulations about flying over the island," Meisner grumbled. "A thorough search in a helicopter could have saved us a lot of wasted energy."

"That's the last thing I'd have expected to hear from an old-schooler like you, Clark," the woman confessed. "I would have thought you'd be the first to respect the tribes' beliefs concerning aerial intrusion. Never mind that chopper reconnaissance is sacrilege to any overlander worth his pith helmet."

"Touché," Meisner said, unsheathing his machete. "Okay, let's push on," he told their guide. Juan Jaisez, a short, wiry man scarred about the face and arms from a lifetime of trailblazing, turned and passed along Meisner's message in the native tongue of the dozen Roiyad tribesmen accompanying the expedition.

Of the five known sects inhabiting the tropical jungles of Skyler's Island, the Roiyad dwelt closest to the coast and had the most contact with those transplanting the twentieth century onto otherwise timeless soil. Though more receptive to newcomers than some of the other tribes, the Roiyad had been slow to adopt Western ways and, in sharp contrast to the khaki outfits and sturdy leather boots worn by the expedition leaders, the natives were content to brave the elements barefoot and clad only in sparse loincloths. Half of them carried canvas-wrapped packs filled with foodstuffs and other supplies, including photographic gear and the tranquilizer guns with which they would hopefully subdue the objects of Meisner's quest. The other six men brandished machetes and had the job of inching past Meisner and Tyne before chopping at thick, ropelike lianas and other dense foliage slowing their progress.

They resumed carving out a narrow swath, so as to do the least damage to the natural environment, and the group forged on in single file. Jaisez kept a protective grip on his Baikal Model MC-21, a 12-gauge shotgun with a checkered walnut finish, while Tyne's 20-gauge, double-barrel Beretta Model 424 was slung over her shoulder and a Ruger Standard Automatic rested on her hip in a polished leather holster. Aside from his machete, Meisner was armed only with an old Pentax LX camera, with which he hoped to shoot at least one wild spectacled kouprey before it was downed by a tranquilizer charge.

As they waded through the overgrowth, Jaisez and Tyne both waved their double-barrels back and forth, peering through the greenery, guarding against the remote chance that a stalking jaguar might catch their scent and consider the group a welcome change from its accustomed diet of tapirs and capybaras.

After another half hour of painstaking progress, they finally came upon a small clearing near the edge of a narrow tributary. Only dappled shards of sunlight penetrated the thick canopy of crowded trees and Meisner had to consult with his watch to confirm that it was high noon.

"Let's take a breather," he announced, sheathing his machete and unslinging his camera from around his neck before crouching with Tyne near the base of a nearby tree. Jaisez informed the Roiyad, who moved as a group to the stream's edge and splashed water onto their gleaming ebony torsos before they formed a tight circle and began murmuring to one another in what seemed to be a repetitive, mantralike chant.

"They're praying for clear weather the rest of the journey," Jaisez told Tyne and Meisner as he leaned against another tree and began rolling a cigarette. Although born in South America, Jaisez had spent all but two of his forty-one years either in the States or working for Americans, so there was only the faintest hint of ancestry in his accent. "We're in a flood plain now and they're afraid that a sudden storm will drown us all."

"Not much chance of that," Meisner said. "They say the next rain front won't be moving in for another five days."

"These folks don't believe in weather forecasts." Jaisez lit up and blew smoke on his arms, warding off a swarm of gnats. "It's all up to the gods in their book. If somebody up there decides we need to be punished, whoosh, we'll have a monsoon."

Tyne snickered. "Well, I'm glad I've done nothing that warrants punishment then."

"You certainly haven't," Meisner told her admiringly. "I have to admit, I had my doubts that you'd be up for the rigors of an expedition like this, but you've more than held your own."

"My, my, aren't we being a little chauvinistic?"

"No, it's not that," Meisner said. "It's just that, I don't know, somehow I didn't think jungle training would be something a CIA agent would have either the time or inclination for."

"Then you underestimate the Agency," Tyne told him. "And you forget some of the places where we do business. Trust me, when you're on assignment in Nicaragua or some place even closer to the tropics, you don't expect to get the job done slinking around in a trench coat."

"I suppose you wouldn't," Meisner conceded.

"If you want to know the truth," Tyne said, "*I* was worried about *you*."

"Me?"

"Yeah, you. I mean, you admitted yourself it had been more than three years since you'd been out in the field, and roaming some outdoor zoo in Miami hardly seemed like enough of a challenge to keep someone in shape."

"Well, I guess we're both just full of surprises." Meisner turned his attention momentarily to his camera, unscrewing the lens cap and using a strip of soft cloth to gently brush away bits of dust and dirt that had somehow lighted on the glass. In the process, he happened to glance to his right, his eyes suddenly widening. "Mother of God," he whispered.

"What?" Jaisez tossed his cigarette and instinctively clenched his shotgun.

"There!"

Meisner led Tyne and Jaisez to the soft loam near the river's embankment. Imbedded in the ground were several distinctive hoofprints and, several yards away, flies buzzed around a small stool left behind by the beast who'd tracked across the loam.

"Kouprey?" Jaisez asked.

Meisner crudely gauged the size of the prints with his fingers, then resorted to a small manual taken from his back pocket. Once he'd compared one of the prints with a page in the booklet, he let out an exultant whoop. "Yes! I'm sure of it."

"Well, what do you know?" Tyne told him. "Congratulations."

"Not yet," Meisner said, aiming his camera at the prints and snapping several quick pictures. "Wait until we have a chance to follow these tracks. Then we'll... Damn these gnats!"

Meisner slapped at his neck, expecting to crush one of the small pests. Instead, he came away holding a small, feather-tufted projectile no longer than his thumbnail. There was blood on his fingers from where the dart had pierced his skin.

"Shit!" Jaisez cursed once he saw the barb-tipped object in Meisner's hand. "Doteine!"

Even as the dreaded word was leaving the guide's lips, it was being repeated by the Roiyad tribesmen, who were lunging to their feet and staring about wildly. One of them stood numbly in place, staring at the thin tendril of blood streaming down his chest from where he'd just pulled loose another of the darts.

Across the river, the jungle suddenly came alive with a chorus of loud, frenzied shouts, and soon there appeared a handful of lean men whose faces and torsos were streaked with bands of vivid red and purple. Those not firing at the expedition with long bamboo blowguns were placing arrows into their longbows and pulling the drawstrings taut. The first of the unleashed shafts thudded loudly into the tree behind Tyne and Meisner, while a second projectile drew an anguished cry from the Roiyad whose abdomen it had pierced.

Tyne unholstered her automatic and handed her 424 to Meisner while Jaisez leveled his shotgun at the Doteine, discharging both barrels and felling two warriors who were attempting to charge across the shallow stream. The men crumpled under the impact of the 12-gauge blasts, landing hard in the water as their companions held back along the distant bank.

"Let's get out of here!" Jaisez shouted to Tyne and Meisner. There was no need for him to translate for the Roiyad, who were already taking flight back down the raw trail they'd created only moments earlier.

Tyne fired a round from her automatic at the Doteine, but Meisner hesitated, not only out of reluctance but also because the effects of his dart wound were already mushrooming. The shotgun felt incredibly heavy in his weakening arms and his vision blurred, doubling the number of warriors screaming their rage at him and the rest of the expedition party.

"Come on!" Tyne grabbed Meisner by the arm and pulled him to one side a split second before an arrow whistled through the air where he'd been standing. The explorer dropped his shotgun and staggered through the mud. Tyne continued to coax him along.

"My eyes," he gasped hoarsely. "I can barely see . . . or breathe."

"Poison dart." She urged him on. "We've got to get you back to the boat. Hang on."

Meisner concentrated as best he could on running, but he felt as if the commands from his brain were being diverted en route to his arms and legs, and it was difficult for him to retain his balance. Tyne called out to Jaisez, who dropped back and helped support Meisner. With the way back to their boat already cleared, it would normally have taken them a fraction of the time they'd spent reaching the point of the ambush, but as Meisner continued to weaken from the poison coursing through his system, the expedition was forced to slow its pace. Fortunately, blasts from Jaisez's Baikal and Tyne's automatic had dissuaded the Doteine from pursuing their assault beyond the branch of the river where they'd surprised their intended victims.

ONCE THE ROIYAD and the expedition leaders vanished back down the trail, two of the painted warriors silently continued to follow them through the brush. The others remained back on the far side of the river, smiling proudly at the effect of their territorial defense. A few of the men even began to laugh.

And out in the middle of the stream, the two attackers who had supposedly fallen under the bite of Jaisez's Baikal slowly rose from the water. The trail of red that flowed down their bodies was that of their war paint, not blood. Neither man bore so much as the slightest hint of a bullet wound. As they waded back to the embankment, their cohorts reached out to help them ashore. One of them chuckled. "That should give us a little privacy for a while, yes?"

He spoke, not in the tongue of the true Doteine or any other native tribesmen of Skyler's Island, but in Spanish.

Like the others, he was a Colombian.

2

"Hard to believe it's been over a year already," Gadgets Schwarz said as he stared out at the Municipal Stadium ball field in West Palm Beach, where the Montreal Expos' minor-league prospects struggled to hold a narrow lead over the visiting Jacksonville team.

"You know what they say," Sandy Meisner told him between bites of her chili dog. "Time sure flies when you're under the gun."

Schwarz chuckled. "Oh? And when did they start saying that?"

"My first assignment, as I remember."

"Well, I don't know about you, but as long as I'm taking a breather, I'd rather hold off on the shop talk," Schwarz said. "For the next four days the only gun I want to see is the one they use behind the plate to time fastballs."

"Fair enough." Sandy reached for her beer and held it out, as if in a toast. "To a genuine vacation," she proposed.

"And to good company to share it with," Gadgets added. "Cheers."

They tapped cups and sipped their beer, turning back to watch the game. Fortunately they both were finding it relatively easy to shake off the heavy burdens that came with their jobs and to enjoy themselves. For Sandy this was a long way from the drug wars she fought regularly along the Florida coast on behalf of the DEA. And Gadgets felt far removed from his responsibilities as part of Able Team, a three-man counterterrorist squad operating out of Stony Man Farm in Virginia, where they more often than not received their battle orders from the man who lived at 1600 Pennsylvania Avenue in the nation's capital.

Ironically he and Sandy had first crossed paths at this same ballpark the previous spring, due to a mutual interest in the plight of former Dodger great Doug Bendix. The retired baseball player's postretirement woes had inadvertently drawn him into a web of international intrigue centered around attempts by organized crime to set up a major heroin network at a sugarcane refinery Bendix was part owner of. In the process of vindicating Bendix, who was now coaching third base for the Jacksonville team, Gadgets and Sandy had both witnessed and taken part in the spilling of criminal blood all the way from Palm Beach down to Miami, and their collaboration had proved to be one of pleasure, as well as business. At the end of that assignment they had left the door open for an eventual resumption of their relationship, but it had taken longer than anticipated for them to coordinate a rendezvous. They'd already spent one festive night together and were looking forward to a weekend of more of the same.

But for now baseball was the diversion of choice. Unlike last spring, when Schwarz had donned a glove and uniform to participate in a celebrity baseball camp, he was now content to be a mere spectator. It was fate that chose to draw him into the action when, moments later, the batter leaned into an inside slider and pulled it down the third-base line, over Bendix's head in the coach's box and toward the stands. Quickly setting down his beer, Schwarz leaned halfway across Sandy's knees and extended his left arm outward. The ball slapped loudly into his callused palm and he closed his fingers quickly, willing himself to ignore the deep sting of the catch. Turning slightly in Sandy's lap, he grinned up at her and proudly held out the ball, announcing to her and the several dozen other fans within earshot, "Ta da!"

He received a small ovation and Bendix cupped his hands around his mouth as he hollered, "Sign that boy up, pronto!"

"Sorry," Schwarz shouted back, "but I'm already in the big leagues. Different sport, though."

A row back from Schwarz and Sandy was a freckle-faced girl wearing an Expos ball cap and a first baseman's glove that looked like a lobster's claw on her small hand. When Gadgets placed the ball in her glove she thanked him profusely and dashed off to impress her friends.

"That was nice of you," Sandy told him.

"I always wanted to do that," he confessed.

The next pitch whistled by the batter for a called third strike, ending the game. As players from both teams cleared their benches to exchange handshakes and as fans began to file toward the exits, the beeper on Sandy's belt pulsed several times in quick succession.

"Perfect timing," she grumbled, going to her purse to get change for a pay phone. "Sorry, Gadgets, but I need to check in at the office."

"They make you haul around a beeper when you're on vacation?"

"We're expecting an important witness to come out of the woodwork on the toughest case we've tackled all year," she said. "I really didn't figure on it happening this soon, obviously, but if it's them, maybe I can still wrap up my end of things before we take off."

"Go ahead and call," Schwarz told her. "I want to talk to Doug for a minute. I'll catch you by the phones."

"Thanks for understanding."

"I've been there, Sandy," Gadgets assured her. "Look, next time it'll probably be me who gets the call."

Sandy crumpled her hot-dog wrapper into the drained beer cup and let it fly in the general direction of the nearest trash can. It bounced off the aluminum side and landed in the dirt before she could scoop it up for a rebound. Schwarz walked down to the chain-link fence separating the stands from the playing field. Bendix and a couple of Jacksonville players were obliging fans with autographs. As soon as he was free, the veteran walked over to Schwarz.

"Good to see you again, Gadgets."

"Likewise, Doug. Got over that bullet wound?"

Bendix nodded, twisting his torso to demonstrate a full range of motion. During the climax of last year's assignment, both Schwarz and Bendix had found themselves in the middle of a parking-lot shootout behind the stadium, with the ex-ball player taking a hit in the ribs. He tapped the area now and said, "The scar's a little sensitive, but I've got a lady friend to kiss it every night and make it feel better."

"Good."

"Speaking of lady friends, I see you and Sandy have gotten together, just like I predicted."

"Just for the weekend," Schwarz said. "We're heading down to Key West. She wants to buy a kitten at the old Hemingway place."

"Sounds great. And how are the other guys?"

"All in one piece. They're all back up north, resting up for our next assignment."

The other guys were Carl "Ironman" Lyons and Rosario "Pol" Blancanales, his Able Team partners, as well as John Kissinger and Jack Grimaldi, Stony Man Farm's resident weaponsmith and ace pilot, respectively. Together they constituted the heart of a special task force the government called upon to deal with domestic unrest requiring the kind of no-holds-barred treatment more conventional law-enforcement agents were wary of engaging in. And there was plenty of action on that front. After their clash with the drug smugglers in Florida, the group had spent the past year going head-to-head with several renegade KGB operatives, a fanatic San Diego cult leader, assorted hit men in four different states, imported Chinese terrorists and Vegas mob elements. Through it all they'd survived triumphantly with only minimal injuries, but the cumulative exhaustion had finally caught up with them and they'd eagerly grabbed the chance for some down time.

Schwarz and Bendix talked a while longer, then the coach had to excuse himself. Gadgets circled behind the stands to track down Sandy. She had just hung up the phone and had a bleak, stunned look on her face.

"Sandy?" He moved toward her. "Are you okay?"

She looked up at him, pained sadness in her eyes. "I have to go to Miami," she said. "My brother's in the hospital there. They say he's dying...."

IT WAS AN HOUR AND A HALF drive to Miami. On the way Sandy briefed Schwarz on her brother Clark's background and elaborated on how much of an influence and inspiration he had been to her over the years. Between the lines, Gadgets could sense her love for the explorer and also her great anxiety over his uncertain fate. He listened with interest as she described the expedition, in part because he'd often heard Skyler's Island mentioned in an entirely different context than as a possible haven for endangered bovines. The isle often came up in conversations with various intelligence agencies, who couldn't help but note its strategic location in the Caribbean. There were theories that both the Cubans and Russians viewed Skyler's Island as a potentially valuable springboard for troop movements in the event of increased military activity in Central America, but to date no hard evidence had been unearthed to support such suspicions. Still, Schwarz reasoned to himself, if a supposedly extinct breed of wild oxen had eluded detection there all these years, who was to say there weren't other secrets hidden in the heart of the island's jungle interior.

The closer they came to their destination, the less talkative Sandy became, and for the last half hour they rode silently, watching twilight fade across the horizon to give way to the coming night. Soon Miami's coastal sprawl appeared before them, glittering with its millions of lights. Before reaching the city they exited from the turnpike and took side streets to the hospital, a tall, monolithic structure set on a landscaped plot near Opa Locka Airport.

"Let's hope for the best," Schwarz said as they headed for the main entrance.

"He has to be okay," Sandy whispered. "He has to. He's the only family I have left."

Inquiring at the lobby, however, they found out that Clark Meisner's condition was listed as critical, and when a nurse led them to his private room in the intensive-care unit, Sandy's face registered both pain and shock at the sight of the man she'd spent her lifetime looking up to.

The color gone from his face, Meisner's skin had taken on a yellowish, waxy luster, and even the whites of his eyes had dulled considerably. An oxygen mask was strapped over his nose and mouth, and both his arms were taped in order to secure needles connected to the seven different packets of donor blood, anticoagulant drugs, poison serums and other solutions trickling into his system in hopes of maintaining his tenuous grip on life. An EKG monitor tracked the weak, erratic pulse of his heart. But despite his debilitated condition, when he saw his sister walk through the doorway, Meisner managed a faint smile.

"'Lo, Sis," he rasped weakly through his mask, struggling to raise his right hand.

"Hi, Clark," Sandy said, sitting at the edge of the bed and entwining her fingers in his. His cold, clammy touch was unsettling, but she did her best not to show fear.

"I'll just wait outside," Schwarz volunteered, taking a step back toward the doorway.

Meisner feebly shook his head. "That's not necessary."

Gadgets looked at Sandy and from her expression he saw that she wanted him to stay, too. Pulling up a chair, he sat down at the end of the bed, trying his best to be inconspicuous.

"They told me what happened," Sandy informed her brother. "I still can't believe it. All those other expeditions you went on over the years and never any problems, aside from that time you broke your leg in Tasmania... It just doesn't seem fair. Dammit, you were just looking for some stupid cow!"

"Ox," Meisner corrected with a slight grin. *"Bos sauveli ornatus."*

"You and your damn Latin!" Sandy glanced up at the row of dangling bags dripping their contents down clear tubes to the intravenous needles in his arms. "Why do they have all these? Can't they just give you an antidote?"

"They tried," Meisner told her, swallowing hard between every few words, "but I'm not responding. They can't figure out... what kind of poison."

"Why not?" Sandy gasped with frustration. "This is supposed to be the best poison-control center in the entire South!"

"Can't blame them... they're trying."

Sandy stroked her brother's hand. Noticing feverish beads of perspiration on his forehead, she reached for a tissue and wiped them off. "I still don't understand how it could have happened," she said. "You told me you checked and double-checked the lay of the land there to make sure you wouldn't stray into Doteine territory. You said you wouldn't be anywhere near their turf."

"I didn't think we were," Meisner whispered. He looked at her and smiled. "Sandy. We almost found them."

"Them?"

"The oxen," Meisner said triumphantly. "They're there!"

"Screw the damn oxen!"

Meisner shook his head. Summoning what little strength he had left in him, the explorer tightened his grip on Sandy's hand and sat up in bed. Through his mask, he declared, "No. I want you to *find* the damn oxen!"

"What?" Sandy eased him back. "Clark, you can't be serious!"

"Find the oxen," he repeated, his voice weakening. "For me..."

"Clark, please..."

A nurse came into the room, followed by a pair of doctors and an orderly pushing a tray covered with a variety of syringes and diagnostic instruments. "I'm sorry, but we need to run some more tests. You'll have to leave for a few minutes," one of the doctors requested as he acknowledged Sandy and Gadgets's presence.

Sandy reluctantly rose from the bed, letting go of her brother's hand. His gaze was locked on hers. "Promise," he whispered.

"Clark," she told him hopefully, "when you're better you'll be able to go back there yourself."

"Promise me," he repeated.

She took a deep breath and nodded. "Okay."

The doctors were already preparing for the tests. Gadgets gently placed a hand on Sandy's shoulder and guided her away from the bed. He nodded toward Meisner, then led the woman out into the hallway. She stayed in control until they had rounded the corner to a small alcove where a row of vending machines were lined against a wall. Then, letting out a pent-up sob, she drew close to Schwarz, embracing him as he put his arms around her.

"My God, he looks so sick," she lamented. "I can't believe this is happening."

"He's in good hands," Schwarz told her. "You have to hold on to hope."

"I know, I know." She drew in a deep breath and pulled away from Gadgets, blinking tears from her eyes as she brought herself back under control. "Thanks," she told him. "For being here."

"Glad I can help." Schwarz went through his pockets for some change and went to one of the vending machines. "How about some coffee?"

"Please." While they waited for the first cup to fill, Sandy said, "I know how much finding those oxen meant to him, but they weren't worth this."

"What he said about you going," Schwarz said. "I don't think he really meant it. He's probably a little delirious from the fever."

Sandy sighed, taking the coffee. "Yeah, I think you're right there, but I couldn't refuse him."

When Schwarz's cup was ready, they backtracked to a waiting area just down the hall from Meisner's room and sat down. Schwarz turned to her. "Besides, like you said, once they pinpoint the poison and get him the right antidote, he'll probably be back there in no time and—"

He was interrupted by a message coming over the hospital intercom.

"Code blue, ICU," the dispassionate female voice sounded over the speakers on the wall. "Code blue, ICU."

"Oh God..." Sandy set down her cup and bolted from the chair. Schwarz caught up with her and held her back as the nearby elevator doors whooshed open and a team of hospital personnel hurried out, pushing a portable defibrillation machine between them and heading into the intensive-care wing. Sandy and Schwarz followed as far as the doorway and watched as the crew filed into Meisner's room. She reached for Gadgets's hand and clenched it tightly as they stared at the vague shadows on the other side of the drawn shades.

Three minutes passed, during which several other doctors hurried into the room. None emerged. Sandy bit at her lower lip, fighting back more tears and trying to find consolation in the fact that there had been no further "code blue" announcements. And then the door to Meisner's room opened and the doctors and orderlies began to exit. The solemn looks on their faces told of the outcome.

"No," Sandy whimpered, burying her face in Gadgets's shoulder. "No..."

3

The standoff was in its second hour.

Four gunmen were stationed near windows set in each wall of an unfinished cement-block building set off in the middle of a grassy clearing. They wore brown ski masks, dark gray outfits and each held an Uzi submachine gun in one hand and a palm-sized, push-button detonator in the other. The devices were capable of detonating explosive charges that dangled over the heads of three hostages who had been herded together into the center of the room. Those outside the building had been warned that even if they were able to somehow storm the compound, they could not take out the gunmen without the explosives being triggered. That action would spell gruesome death and dismemberment for the hostages and anyone else within a fifty-yard radius.

Inside the structure, Aaron Kurtzman felt a too-familiar rage. Bound to his wheelchair by taut, knotted lengths of electrical cord, he was useless. Dammit, he thought, if he only had the use of his legs, he could squirm enough to get his feet on the ground and then use his weight to overturn the chair. Granted, he would probably be shot point-blank for such a maneuver, but the distraction might be sufficient to buy some time for the rescue squad huddled outside. His death under such circumstances would not be in vain—it could possibly lead to the rescue of the other hostages, prominent Middle Eastern leaders who had come to this remote meeting place in hopes of hammering out a peace accord in that turbulent corner of the globe.

But such musings were little more than an exercise in futility because Kurtzman was hopelessly immobile, trapped in the small motorized vehicle that had been his only source of locomotion since being paralyzed by a bullet wound to the spine some six years ago. It had been the gun blast of a traitor that had felled him back then, and to once again find himself compromised by a band of turncoats was a bitter irony that only served to darken the man's already black mood. He longed to curse his captors, but like the other hostages his mouth was tightly gagged.

The roof over their heads was only half-completed, and through a wide opening Kurtzman had a view of the afternoon sky. Small white clouds drifted past like puffs of cotton being carried along by a clear blue current, occasionally obscuring the warm spring sun. Despite, or perhaps because of the dire nature of his predicament, Kurtzman found himself thinking of his childhood back in Chicago, when he had spent many an idle summer day lying in the backyard with his brother, watching cloud formations and seeing who could pick out the most discernible shapes. There's a camel...and that one over there's a whale—no, wait, it's...it's...a fat ballerina. Yeah, a real tubber, like Becky Newhall. Innocent games in an innocent time, when his notion of fighting crime was restricted to playful games of cops and robbers during which death by cap pistol was an unbloody and temporary phenomenon.

He'd had no way of knowing back then that the real weapons of the world ravaged flesh and tissue with brutal force, and that those victims who were lucky enough to survive had to contend with physical and emotional scars lasting far longer than the few minutes it took to wait for one game to finish and another to begin.

Just as Kurtzman was about to draw his gaze away, he saw a small plane course through the sky far above the building. Then two tiny specks fell out into the open air like seeds springing from a pod. Moments later, as the plane flew beyond his view, he was able to see the unfurling of two parachutes and the slow downward descent of what he could now recognize as two men, one of them carrying an assault rifle and the other something roughly the size and shape of a cigar box.

Good move, Kurtzman thought to himself as he diverted his upward gaze so that he wouldn't tip off the captors. It's exactly the strategic ploy he would have authorized under such circumstances, although he would have covered the parachutists' approach by stepping up activity on the ground to keep the kidnappers occupied and—

As if responding to his mental cue, a sudden series of staccato blasts sounded from the clearing, and the captors leaned closer to their window outposts and returned fire with their Uzis. The hostages next to Kurtzman cringed in the chairs they were bound to, but he concentrated every fiber of his being on a more constructive reaction. In direct proportion to the uselessness of his legs, Kurtzman had weight-trained his upper body into a muscular physique, and he focused his considerable strength in an effort to rock his wheelchair from side to side. Heavy as he was, it took only three attempts before he was able to shift his weight enough to one side that one wheel rose from the floor and he felt himself falling into the grip of gravity. Instead of tensing, he tried his best to relax as he toppled sideways to the floor with a sharp thud. His right shoulder bore the brunt of the fall and he felt merciless jolts of pain rush through his body from the point of impact, but he was able to retain consciousness and witness the fruit of his labors.

As expected, the moment he fell, two of the gunmen paused to look back at him. One of them promptly let out a howl as an incoming bullet from one of the ground forces caught him off guard and he collapsed against the wall, dropping his detonator. The other man swung his Uzi at Kurtzman and took a long stride toward him. When he was halfway to the hostages, a shadow briefly swept across the floor, and by the time the terrorist glanced up to see what had caused it, Pol Blancanales was floating down through the huge opening in the roof and landing hard only a few feet away from him. Rolling on impact, Pol bowled the gunman over and came up cradling a Colt Commando submachine gun in his hands. Without fully rising to his feet, the chutist, who had distinguished himself as a paratrooper during his tours in Vietnam, leveled his weapon at the remaining gunmen and fired.

Two of the other captors went down under his fusillade, but the remaining man managed to dive toward the hostages and use them as a shield. Letting out a cry in what sounded like Arabic, the man pressed his detonator and closed his eyes in anticipation of the explosion that would express-deliver him to Allah. Kurtzman saw the button being pushed and likewise braced himself for doom. But, to both men's surprise, the charge didn't take. Kurtzman heard the second parachutist land on the roof and immediately he surmised that the man must be carrying a transmitter that had somehow managed to override the detonator's radio signal.

Good work, Carl, he thought, knowing that the man had to be Carl Lyons, the blond Californian who served as Able Team's battlefield strategist. And sure enough, Lyons appeared moments later, freed of his parachute and leaping through the gap in the roof to a spot between the hostages and the last surviving captor. With an effortless series of quick but powerful shotokan karate blows, Lyons disarmed the gunman and rendered him unconscious.

And so the siege was over.

Lyons hurried over to Kurtzman's side and removed the man's gag before helping to right his wheelchair.

"Nice of you guys to drop in." Kurtzman chuckled at his rescuers.

"What the hell, we were in the neighborhood," Lyons wisecracked as he began untying Kurtzman's arms and torso.

Blancanales, unhitching himself from his parachute, went to one of the windows and waved for the ground forces to hold fire, then joined Lyons near the hostages and started untying knots. "All in a day's work," he said.

Off in the corner, unnoticed by the rescue party, one of the terrorists stirred and slowly sat up. Although there were huge red splotches on the man's chest where he'd taken direct hits from Blancanales's Colt Commando, the man showed no sign of pain or weakness. His Uzi lay only a few feet away, easily within reach. But instead of reaching for the gun, the man did a strange thing.

He clapped.

"Well done, boys," he called out cheerily. "You've made an old man proud."

"Thanks, Chief," Lyons said with a laugh. "But I don't think you're that old."

The would-be terrorist yanked off his ski mask to reveal himself as none other than Hal Brognola, Stony Man Farm's director of operations. As he cast aside the mask and reached inside his paint-splattered jacket for a cigar, the other terrorists also rose from the dead and shed their disguises. Jack Grimaldi, the Farm's resident pilot, and Walt Newark and Mel Flynn of the compound's security detail, came over to help Lyons and Blancanales untie the three guards who had posed as the captive negotiators.

"Only one change that I'd suggest," Brognola said, lighting up his cigar. "I would have had someone on a bullhorn talking a blue streak to mask the sound of the plane."

"We considered that," Lyons said, "but I figured that the longer we had someone talking, the more suspicious you'd be that we were up to something with the plane. Judgment call."

"Good point," Brognola conceded. "But I think the plane was still a bit too much of a tip-off, low as you had to bring it in."

The group continued to discuss other aspects of the simulated raid as they wrapped up the exercise, which had taken place inside the framework for the partially completed gymnasium located just a short walk from the main house that served as headquarters for the Stony Man operation. Although Able Team had participated in more successful rescue missions and assignments than any other outfit in the U.S. military or intelligence community, it was not their nature to rest on their laurels, and exercises such as this were standard procedure during those lull periods between assignments. In a profession where instinct was everything, it was worthwhile to ensure that those instincts were well honed and reliable. The day's mission had been reassuring on that front.

"And now that you've earned your keep," Brognola said as they left the construction site and headed across the clearing to the main house, "why don't you all take the rest of the day off?"

There was widespread cheering that spread to the other security officers outside the building who had participated in the drill.

"I say we grab some grits, kick back and catch some of the play-offs," Blancanales said. "I got a feeling the Pistons are going to give the Lakers problems this time around...."

AS IT TURNED OUT, the Lakers were hot and Detroit was reeling on the ropes by halftime, having been outgunned by twenty-four points. The men were watching the game on a wide-screen television in the headquarters den, helping themselves to the spread of cold cuts and other dishes laid out by the staff cook.

"Not bad," Lyons commented, turning his head to make sure that no one from the kitchen could hear them, "but I'll take one of Vinnie's roast beef triple-deckers anytime."

"I'm with you there, Ironman," Blancanales conceded as he washed down his pastrami-on-rye with a long swig of Canadian ale. "But Hobbs is pretty set back in Vegas and I don't think there's gonna be any way he'll find us more attractive than that showgirl he just married."

"Oh, I don't know," Grimaldi wisecracked, rolling up his pant cuffs. "I've got a good set of legs, if you don't pay too much attention to the scars."

"Somehow it's not quite the same thing, Jack," Pol told him.

Vince Hobbs was Stony Man Farm's former chef and gardener, who had resettled in his native Las Vegas. Able Team had flown out to attend his wedding a few weeks ago, only to be drawn into one of their more dangerous assignments when Hobbs's young nephew had become the target of a mob hit man. By the time the men had saved the day, they'd found themselves butting heads with a band of skinhead white suprem-acists, a poison-slavering gila monster and a renegade crime syndicate trying to set up shop in the glitter city. Coming back to Virginia after that encounter, the men had relished their time off. Schwarz had already headed down to Florida the day before, and the other men had various plans for the coming week, after which they were slated to do some high-level protec-tion work during a visit by various Middle Eastern leaders in Washington. Today's exercise had been geared toward preparation for that assignment.

"Uh-oh," Lyons murmured when the side door to the den opened and Hal Brognola poked his head in from the communications room. "Chief, you've got that sorry-boys-but-it-looks-like-vacation's-over look."

"Is it that obvious?" Brognola queried.

"Afraid so."

"Well, what can I say?" Brognola shrugged and tapped ash from his cigar into a nearby tray. "Sorry, boys, but it looks like vacation's over. Come on in and we'll talk about it."

The adjacent communications room was roughly the same size as the den but far less inviting. The huge walnut table and government-issue chairs reeked of business, and as the men filed into the room and sat down they all had a wary sense of the inevitable.

"Okay, Chief, so where are we going this time?" Lyons drawled.

"Someplace new," Brognola said.

"You're kidding, right?" Lyons glanced at a map posted on the wall behind him. "Seems to me we've covered damn near every state in the union since we signed up on this gig."

"And you're probably right on that count," Brognola conceded. "But this time you're in for a change of place, not to mention pace."

Grimaldi moaned. "Don't tell me...Siberia?"

Brognola smiled ruefully and shook his head. "Not even close." Instead of sitting down with the others, he went over to the map and jabbed his index finger into the Caribbean Sea. "Does the name Skyler's Island mean anything to any of you?"

Kurtzman wheeled in from the nearby computer room with a stack of readouts in his lap. As he began passing them around to the other men, he said, "This should help jog your memories."

Blancanales, who had Puerto Rican ancestry in his blood, ignored the handout and told Brognola, "Yeah, I know the place. I had a cousin back in P.R. and whenever he got out of line his old man always threatened to ship him out to Skyler's Island with the next batch of prisoners."

"You must be talking ancient history, Pol, because they shut that penal colony down nearly thirty years ago," Grimaldi said.

"Maybe that's what made it so scary," Pol surmised. "I remember stories about how some of the prisoners escaped into the jungle and got the natives to think they were messengers from the gods."

Kurtzman chuckled as he took his place at the table. "I doubt that was the case, but I bet it kept your cousin in line."

"Never mind that," Grimaldi interrupted. "What's going on down there that would concern us?"

"Something that has to do with Schwarz, I'll bet," Lyons wisecracked. "I knew we shouldn't have let him get out of our sights."

"As a matter of fact, you're right," Kurtzman said, "at least partially."

"Which part?"

"Okay, everyone," Brognola said, taking control of the meeting. "Let me lay out the facts for you."

Referring to the notes Kurtzman had passed around, Brognola brought the group up-to-date on Schwarz's hospital visit to Clark Meisner and the curious mission that Sandy Meisner had decided to undertake on her slain brother's behalf. "Normally," he went on, "I wouldn't consider this a matter of concern for the Farm, but there are some other variables here that make it business."

Grimaldi snapped his fingers, remembering something. "Now I know where I've heard that place mentioned. It's on the Agency's shit list of places where the Communists could be setting up clandestine training bases, right?"

"Yeah, I remember that, too," Lyons piped in, grinning to himself as he stole a sidelong glance at Kurtzman's notes. "And wasn't there something about some Vesco-type guy? Hooker something?"

"Hokes," Brognola said. "Stephen Hokes. He left the mainland two years ago with nearly a billion and a half dollars worth of swindled booty and promptly dropped out of sight. Word is he's cut a deal with the powers-that-be on Skyler's Island, putting up bribe money in exchange for sanctuary."

"I hate fuckers like that," Lyons snapped irritably.

"Good," Brognola said, "because from the sounds of it, you just might have a chance to tell it to his face."

4

Stephen Hokes was awakened shortly after sunrise by the gentle hands of Murielta, the eighteen-year-old Thiglada tribeswoman he'd acquired as a personal servant shortly after moving onto the 543-acre Skyler's Island plantation he now called his home. She hummed softly to rouse him from his slumber as she parted the curtains of his canopied bed, and as the remnants of a dream faded from his mind, Hokes smiled contentedly and rolled onto his back beneath the silk sheets. His movement made it easier for the thin, supple-limbed woman to brush her fingers across the soft white flesh of his abdomen down to his loins. He was already hard and waiting for her willing lips to greet him.

"Ah, good morning, Murielta," he whispered as he ran his fingers through her long black hair.

She'd long ago learned the way to please him, and she performed the daily ritual with deft prowess, flicking her tongue artfully and fondling him with tender caresses. She smiled briefly at his final moan.

Her task completed, Murielta silently withdrew from the bed and padded across the Persian rug to a spacious bathroom, where she began to draw hot water into a tiled tub that was almost as large as the man's bed. Adding a small handful of scented bath beads, she slowly stirred the water with her hand, creating a thick cover of suds.

Hokes cast aside his covers and slipped on a bathrobe as he crossed the room to a doorway that opened onto a small terrace. Stepping outside, he stood at the railing and took in a deep breath of morning air and looked around with satisfaction. The mansion, set roughly in the middle of the plantation grounds, had been built to demanding specifications, including Hokes's desire that *his* land would be all that one viewed for as far as the eye could see in any direction. And so it was. Stretching out before him were the landscaped grounds and his personal polo field, and beyond that the stables where his prized thoroughbreds were kept.

Far off in the distance were the scattered buildings and barracks where the harvesters and his work crew lived, and rising up against the horizon were the rubber trees that accounted for that portion of his income that he chose to make public to the government officials of Skyler's Island. Of course, although rubber brought him a fortune that would dazzle the minds of most individuals, in reality it constituted only a fraction of his full income and worth. Since arriving on the island six years ago, he'd expanded upon the business connections he'd made before his flight from the States, and in conjunction with his present circle of associates, Hokes dealt in many commodities that he wasn't about to list in his portfolio.

One such business transaction was scheduled to take place this morning, and as he lit a cigarette and stared out at the overcast skies above the island, Hokes heard the faint, distant drone of an aircraft. Reaching for a pair of high-powered binoculars, he focused on a point to the southwest, where the thickest growth of rubber trees marked a boundary between his land and the neighboring jungle. Moments later, an ancient DC-3 dropped into view below the cloud cover, powered by its twin Pratt-Whitney fourteen-cylinder engines. Over the past five decades the plane had logged tens of thousands of flight hours under various pretenses, but none quite like the missions for which it had been flying the past seven weeks.

Once Hokes had the DC-3 in his sights, he followed its course over the jungle, whispering a countdown under his breath.

"...four...three...two...one...zero."

As if on his cue, small bomblike specks began to drop from the underbelly of the aircraft, and as they plummeted, each of the parcels sprang a parachute, breaking their fall into the jungle. In all, thirteen pieces of cargo made the drop, then the DC-3 banked to the right and gained altitude until it was once again swallowed by the thick bank of clouds and gone from sight. As planned, the majority of the parcels landed in open clearings on Hokes's property, but three parachutes drifted slightly off course, taking their loads into the verdant density of the jungle.

"Shit," Hokes said, setting aside the binoculars. He took one last drag of his cigarette, then flicked it over the railing and wandered back inside. There was a shortwave radio sitting on an antique French desk in the corner, and Hokes used it to pass along word of the errant packages. He was assured that the drop had been witnessed by the necessary parties and that all thirteen parcels would be secured and brought to the processing plant forthwith.

"Good," Hokes said, turning off the radio and opening one of the desk drawers to pull out a palm-sized mirror heaped high with a fine white powder. With a razor blade he carefully portioned off two thin lines and inhaled them through a trimmed straw, one line up each nostril. Almost immediately he could feel his momentary anxiety being numbed by the cool, anesthetic rush of the cocaine. He ran the straw along the front of his gums, tasting the medicinal bitterness of what little residue he had failed to sniff.

Next to his bed, Hokes had a three-thousand-dollar sound system, and he sorted through his collection of compact disks until he found a selection that struck his fancy. Some vintage Steve Winwood.

"Bring me a higher love," he crooned happily as he turned up the volume and bobbed his head in time with the music. In the other room, Murielta had just lowered herself into the steaming waters of the bath, and Hokes smiled as he cast aside his bathrobe and climbed down so that he was sitting in front of her, legs outstretched, his shoulders pressed against the soft cushion of her breasts. She kissed the back of his head and reached around him with a bar of soap, beginning to lather the thick mat of hair on his chest. "Yes," he murmured contentedly. "Ain't this the life...."

ALMOST FIVE HUNDRED YARDS away from Hokes's mansion, Bernardo Octria responded to the dropping packages and the subsequent call from Hokes by ramming a fresh 14-round magazine into his Smith & Wesson Model 59. He quickly led his six Colombian underlings from the guest house they had made their home since arriving on Skyler's Island more than three months ago. The other men were armed with mini-Uzis and machetes and were equally adept with both weapons, having had ample opportunity and necessity to use both during the years they had helped lord over the Mibyche Cartel's South American-based cocaine empire.

In its prime, the Cartel had undoubtedly been one of the most influential and feared organizations in the drug world. Intramural squabblings and infiltration by undercover law-enforcement agencies had dealt the Cartel a crippling blow the previous winter. In fact, it was only through a stroke of good fortune that Octria's small band of men had managed to leave their native land mere hours before a vengeful hit squad had converged upon one of the mountain enclaves where the precious coca leaves underwent the processing that extracted the valued drug for the smuggling trade. Now, several hundred miles away, the Colombians hoped to rebuild their crumbled operation and once again share in the untold wealth to be earned through the trafficking of illicit substances.

At the far end of the plantation, close to the first rows of mature rubber plants, the seven men strode past a fellow Colombian guarding the entrance to a decrepit old barn that had once been the primary structure of the land's previous tenants. Gone were the days when horses and cattle were kept in the barn, however. Now the hay-strewn stalls were lined with crude wooden bunks and served as the living quarters for thirty-one lean Thiglada tribesmen, constituting the backbone of the plantation's labor force. Captured during clandestine jungle raids along the periphery of the Thiglada tribe's borders, the men lived the lives of slaves, with their days organized for them by Octria or one of Hokes's plantation foremen in charge of the rubber-harvesting operations. Their families back in the interior had no idea of their fate, although on several occasions search parties had reached as far as the plantation only to be intercepted and repelled by fierce volleys of gunfire.

The natives woke from their sleep to the sound of Octria's shrill whistle, and although their work-weary frames begged for more rest, they knew better than to ignore the call to work. Scrambling from their bunks, where they slept six to a stall, the men fell into a semblance of attention in the middle of the barn. One of their number had curried favor with the Colombians by attempting to bridge their language gap. He served as a crude interpreter for Bernardo, announcing the day's assignment. It was expected that, like so many mornings before, the slaves would be given their tools and be marched out into the seemingly endless fields. They normally spent the next ten hours making spiral slashes in the rubber trees and anchoring the cups that would collect dripping latex for transfer to the processing plant on the north end of the plantation.

Today, however, their interpreter told them the schedule would be different.

The DC-3 was droning in and out of the clouds overhead as the natives filed out of the barn, and more than half of the parachutes were still visible, floating down like the caps of silk mushrooms. Those cargo loads landing in view of the men thudded dully on the savanna grass of the clearing, while the three stray parcels raised cries from the smaller creatures of the jungle as they crashed through the canopy of trees. There were nervous murmurings as the Thigladas speculated as to the meaning of the strange forms sent down by the much-feared bird of silver and thunder. When it was made clear that they were to enter the jungle and track down the missing packages, several of the men dropped to their knees and began to wail disconsolately. It took a harsh slap across the shoulders with the flat of a machete blade for the Colombians to coax the wailers to their feet.

Half of the Colombians headed off with a dozen tribesmen to gather up the goods that had landed in the clearing while Octria led the rest of the group into the jungle. Fortunately, one of the deviant loads had become snagged in a tree, and the collapsed parachute clearly marked the direction they would have to take.

Passage through the rubber trees was effortless, given the neat-rowed symmetry with which they had been planted and the carpetlike smoothness of the surrounding grassland. But when they reached the jungle, the way became instantly forbidding, even along those rare stretches where paths had been hacked only a few days ago. Here in the tropics, where the flora grew rampantly and unchecked, today's well-cleared trail was invariably tomorrow's impregnable corridor. Progress was slow, and the Colombians had to space themselves out in such a way that they could keep an eye on all the slaves, not only to ensure that they wouldn't try to flee, but also that they wouldn't fall by the wayside out of exhaustion from the effort of trudging through the foliage.

It took them nearly half an hour to cover a hundred yards of jungle terrain and reach the first parcel, which swung back and forth eerily from parachute strings reaching up to the treetops above. Roughly the size of an upright piano, the bundle was well wrapped in a waterproof tarpaulin and bound by thick tape and ropes made of hemp. While the interpreter told the natives to stay put, Octria strode forward and used his machete to carefully cut through a section of the covering, exposing kilo bricks of cellophane-wrapped white powder. Pure cocaine. More than six hundred pounds of it in this parcel alone.

Once broken down, smuggled into the States or Europe, and cut with milk sugar or any number of other additives, the street value of this one hoard would skyrocket toward the five million dollar mark. Eight of the other bundles also contained cocaine, albeit in smaller quantities of pasty wads that would be sold on the streets as crack, and three packages contained moisture-laden seedlings of the coca plant. Samples tested on the soil of Stephen Hokes's plantation were found to thrive as well as they did in their native South America. Looking to the future, Octria and Hokes foresaw the day when coca would grow with frenzied abandon in the jungles adjacent to the plantation, providing a steady source of product and making theirs a new cartel that would be the rival of any competitors.

But that would come later. For now the preliminary steps needed to be taken. Octria had his interpreter single out the lightest and most agile of the natives and had him come forward to climb the suspended parcel. Once atop the package, the tribesman was given a machete and instructed to sever the parachute lines holding both him and the bundle aloft. The man followed the orders reluctantly, and when the bale dropped five feet to the jungle floor, he was thrown to one side and howled in pain as his shoulder absorbed the brunt of the fall.

"One down," Octria chortled in Spanish to his co-horts, who shared in his laughter at the injured slave. Their levity was short-lived, however. The sun was already beginning to burn through the morning clouds and the Colombians were anxious to finish their task in the jungle before the temperature climbed any higher and roused the populations of unpleasant insects that had driven them half-mad recently when they'd spent five hours waiting to spring their ambush on the expedition party headed by Clark Meisner.

While one of the gunmen stayed behind to guard the cocaine, Octria and the other Colombian forged ahead with the natives, seeking out the other two bundles. The first was easily located just over two hundred yards away, partially torn where it had crashed through the trees. The final package, however, pulled the group more than a quarter mile deeper into the interior, past the telltale markings of the real Doteine tribe. Wary of an altercation with the warriors, Octria and his partner held their guns close by their sides, ready to open fire at the first sign of provocation. They flinched at each uncommon sound filtering through the thickness of the forest, trying to fathom which bestial cries were natural and which might be the calls of hidden enemies in the brush.

Finally, almost an hour and a half after setting out, the expedition came upon the object of their quest, a sofa-size crate filled with coca seedlings. As he broke down the contents into portable sections, Octria made sure that none of the seals had leaked and that each plant was still preserved in such a way as to survive one final transplant. All but a handful of the seedlings passed the inspection.

"Okay, let's get out of here," Octria told his partner once the last of the loads had been transferred onto the backs of the slaves. On the interpreter's cue, the men began trudging back the way they'd come.

Halfway to the second of the downed parcels, there was a sudden, pronounced thrashing in the foliage off to their left. Octria reflexively whipped his Smith & Wesson into firing position, as did the other Colombian. They were expecting the charge of Doteine warriors; but before they had a chance to register their surprise, they realized that their expedition was under assault not by tribesmen, but rather by a spectacled kouprey. The wild ox was apparently both disoriented and frightened, because although the species wasn't known for aggressive behavior especially toward humans, this particular beast charged the row of terrified slaves with its head lowered and its long, curved horn jutting outward.

Before Octria could bury three 9 mm parabellum slugs in the kouprey's thick neck, it had gored two of the natives and was in the process of stomping on the victims with its powerful hooves. Even then, it was necessary for the other Colombian to creep close and let loose with a lethal spray of his Uzi before the ox slowly sank to its knees and then tumbled over onto its side, moaning its anguish. Octria moved in and pressed the barrel of his Model 59 behind the kouprey's ear before pulling the trigger again and putting the beast out of its misery.

"Steaks," he murmured to himself as he nudged the dead beast with his toe. Speaking through the interpreter, he ordered the natives to strip a nearby sapling and fashion it into a makeshift pole that could be used to suspend the kouprey and carry it back to the plantation.

Meanwhile, the two gored victims writhed in agony where the beast had felled them. Blood spilled through their fingers where they tried in vain to cover their wounds. Octria could tell at a glance that neither man was likely to survive a trip back to the mansion, much less to a hospital, and worse, their impassioned cries of pain were echoing through the jungle, drawing as much attention as the gunshots.

Walking over to the two natives, Octria calmly raised his Smith & Wesson and pulled the trigger twice, piercing each man's skull and silencing them forever. He indicated for his partner to keep his Uzi trained on the other tribesmen, then dragged one of the dead men back through the brush to what appeared to be a small, sandy clearing. As soon as the body came in contact with the surface, however, it began to slowly sink. By the time Octria had gone and returned with the second victim, the first was already halfway swallowed by the quicksand. He rolled in the second corpse and returned to the main trail, meeting the uncertain gazes of the trembling natives. He put the fallen parcels onto his own back, then made a waving gesture with his gun and the grim procession resumed. It was going to be a long trip back to the plantation.

5

Memorial services for Clark Meisner were held at Metrozoo on the future site of an outdoor exhibit that, when completed, would be devoted to the wildlife and flora of South America. The more than three hundred people attending the ceremony were standing in front of folding chairs set in long rows on the hard-packed ground. Animal sounds from the neighboring exhibits filtered through the midday air and far off in the distance was the drone of traffic on the Florida Turnpike.

"Clark Meisner called the outdoors his home and it is only fitting that we come here to give him his final due," Gardner Richwell, mustachioed president of the Metrozoo board of directors, intoned solemnly from the speaker's stand. "And it is particularly appropriate that we meet on this particular piece of land. We plan to introduce a motion at our next meeting that we christen this South American exhibit Meisner's Paradise when it opens next summer."

Despite her grief, Sandy smiled faintly at the announcement. Dressed in a black skirt and blouse, she was standing in the front row, with Gadgets at her side. She cast her head downward and wept quietly as the eulogy continued, highlighting moments of her brother's illustrious public career. Her own memories

of Clark were of a more private nature—recollections
of childhood days and sibling rivalries, weekends with
the grandparents in Vero Beach, his attendance at her
college graduation, the time he brought a floral-print
bullet-proof jacket to her in the hospital after she'd
received a glancing gunshot wound during a drug raid
in the Keys. They had shared many a tear and laugh
over the years. And now he was gone.

At the conclusion of Richwell's remarks, a lone vi-
olinist, standing out of view behind a row of mature
palmettos, began to play an obscure concerto by
nineteenth-century Polish composer Henri Wieniaw-
ski, a distant ancestor in the Meisner family tree. It
was a haunting, melodic piece of music, perfectly
capturing the entwined romanticism and melancholy
that had been the spirit of Clark Meisner. Sandy had
heard the concerto hundreds of times over the years.
It was synonymous with family...family that had, one
by one, fallen to the Reaper until now she was the last
surviving bearer of the family name. The realization
overwhelmed her, and as the other mourners began to
slowly file away to one of the zoo's nearby restaurant
facilities, which had been cordoned off as a reception
area, she turned and gratefully leaned into Schwarz's
embrace, sobbing with the most profound sense of
loss.

Schwarz stayed with her until they were the only two
remaining at the site. They sat silently and for some
time they stared across the grounds, where the Wings
of Asia aviary and the African plains exhibit stood out
in sharp contrast to the Miami skyline to the north.
Schwarz noted the contrails of a jet bound for Miami
International and wondered absently whether Lyons
and Blancanales had made it down from Virginia yet.

His feelings for Sandy aside, he couldn't help but feel a sense of expectation at the thought of Able Team going to Skyler's Island. During the early years of their inception they had frequently undertaken assignments overseas, but of late those missions had fallen under the province of the Team's counterpart, Phoenix Force. By his recollection, this would be the first time they had left the mainland since stealing into the rugged coastline of Central America two and a half years ago to help knock out a Moscow-backed missile installation.

Once Sandy felt ready to leave, they started back to the reception area, pausing momentarily while Sandy poured one last cup of liquid fertilizer at the base of a newly planted *Vochysia* tree, the first vegetation to be introduced to the South American exhibit. A plaque bearing Meisner's name had been affixed to the tree's thin trunk, and Sandy slowly ran her fingers along the lettering.

"I won't let you down, Clark," she promised.

Less than a quarter of the guests had remained for the reception, but the restaurant was still crowded, and it took nearly a half hour before Sandy had accepted the condolences of well-wishers. It was only then that she noticed Pol Blancanales and Carl Lyons, who had finally made their way through the throng to meet her. They extended their condolences and apologized for not arriving sooner.

"That's okay," Sandy said. "I'm grateful enough that you're going to come down to the island with me. I still can't believe your boss would allow it."

"Don't worry, he found a couple ways to make it worth his while," Lyons said.

"It's his specialty," Blancanales quipped. "You could be going to the grocery store for a quart of milk and Brognola would find a way to make a mission out of it."

"Grimaldi and Kissinger here?" Schwarz asked, glancing around the room.

"Nope," Lyons told him. "Believe it or not, Cowboy's down with a bad case of the flu. Grimaldi had a few things to take care of with the jets, so he's hanging back, too. They might join us later on if it looks like we'll need 'em."

Stepping outside the restaurant, the foursome broke away from the others and took seats at an outdoor table to discuss their plans for carrying out Clark Meisner's final wish. Sandy referred to a map Lyons had brought along and pointed out the area where they'd been ambushed.

"As you can see from this map," she said, "they were supposedly two miles outside of Doteine territory, but obviously boundaries have changed recently. I think our best bet this time would be to take a water route, probably the Aitacon River. We can make better time and it would keep us well clear of the Doteine."

"Sounds good to me," Lyons said. "I also think it'd be a good idea if we spent a day or two here in the States boning up on our jungle training before we shove off. This is going to be a change from the climate and battlegrounds we're used to."

"Actually, the DEA has a training ground just a few miles inland from here," Sandy said. "The people who manned those raids down in Bolivia rehearsed up there, so it's a perfect place."

"Okay, let's go for that, then."

They began going over other details, mentioning the ulterior missions of looking for Stephen Hokes and signs of Communist training bases. In fact, they were so caught up in their discussion that they didn't notice that Tyne Murray had wandered into their midst until the woman cleared her throat to get their attention.

"I'm sorry," she said, "but I couldn't help but overhearing. You aren't really thinking of going back to Skyler's Island, are you? After what happened?"

"I have to, Tyne," Sandy told her. "You know what my brother wanted."

Tyne nodded. "Of course, I know all that. But, Sandy, I just don't see the risk being worth it. My God, my investors and I lost everything we put into your brother's expedition and we aren't going to tempt fate trying to recoup the costs. Never mind the fact that there's a big tropical storm heading into the Caribbean this week. And all this other talk of Stephen Hokes and Commies in the brush... I'm sorry, but somebody's been leading you guys astray."

Sandy halted this discussion long enough to introduce Tyne to the three men, then went on. "If we take the proper precautions, I don't think we'll run into the same problems you had."

"I appreciate your intentions but, honestly, I think you'd be making an incredible mistake," Tyne insisted. "I've already checked down there about the status of the Doteines and word is they're hell-bent on overthrowing not only the other tribes, but also the white settlements along the coast. The government down there's not likely to authorize another expedition to stir things up more than they already are."

"We've already got clearance on that," Lyons informed the woman.

"How?" Tyne wanted to know.

"Friends high up," Ironman responded cryptically.

There was a vacant chair at the table and Tyne sat down, taking a careful look at the three men with Sandy. "You're not Company people or I'd recognize you," she said. "Are you Bureau? Or DEA?"

"We're confidential," Lyons said.

"Whatever," Tyne said. "I'm telling you, I can save you all a lot of time and risk if you'd only listen to me. Restless natives aside, I can vouch firsthand that if you're going down there to find Stephen Hokes or Communist training grounds you're going to be disappointed."

"How can you be so sure?" Schwarz asked.

"For most of my last five years with the Company I was stationed in the Caribbean," Tyne explained. "We sniffed high and low for clandestine Red activity and I had a file box filled with bogus leads on Hokes when he flew the States. You ask me, *he* planted all those rumors putting him everywhere from Skyler's Island to Saint Croix and ducked out to Switzerland or Algiers."

"Well, if that's the case," Blancanales said, "then we'll be able to focus more on the expedition, which is fine with me."

"Me, too," Sandy said. She looked at Tyne. "Please, just put yourself in my shoes. You and Clark were partners for only a few months. I knew him all my life. This is just too important for me to back down on."

Tyne sighed and offered Sandy and the men a smile of resignation. "Well, I admire your determination, I'll say that much. And I wish you luck, but I also wish you'd reconsider, if only for your own sakes. I'm telling you, I was down there when we were ambushed, and it's a horrifying feeling. And those storms can't be taken too lightly. You get caught up in a jungle flash flood and there's no escape."

"We're used to bucking the odds," Blancanales assured her. "I think we can handle it."

"I hope you're right." Tyne stood up. "Just take care. I can't say I approve of what you're doing, but please let me know if I can be of any help, okay?"

Sandy nodded.

"Nice to meet you, gentlemen," she told Able Team.

"Likewise," Lyons said, locking his gaze on the woman. She stared back at him a moment without her expression changing, then turned and headed back into the reception area.

"Easy, Ironman," Blancanales told Lyons. "I've seen that look in your eye before. You don't even know if she's available."

Lyons grinned. "Yeah, I guess you're right."

The four friends went back to their planning, but Lyons continued to glance in the direction Tyne had headed, waiting for another glimpse of the woman. Pol's warning aside, he hoped to run into her again.

6

Going into his third day of isolation at a nondescript motor inn eleven miles away from Stony Man Farm, John Kissinger was feeling the pangs of cabin fever. A VCR linked up to the television had provided him with some diversion from the boredom, and he even managed a flimsy smile as he watched the madcap antics of the Marx Brothers in *Duck Soup*, but as soon as the movie ended he was once again reminded of his situation and the depression returned. He used the remote control to turn the set off and, throwing off his covers, he straggled to the kitchenette to heat up the kettle for another pot of tea. Even that small amount of exertion was trying and he leaned against the counter to conserve his strength. Next to the sink were bottles of erythromycin, megadose vitamin C, Maximum-Strength Tylenol and golden seal root. He tapped out a handful of pills and capsules and washed them down with orange juice as he waited for the water to heat up.

"Damn flu," he grumbled, cursing the microscopic germs that had given his body a worse beating than years of gunfights and athletic competition combined.

He'd woken up sick the day before, running a fever and feeling a muscle ache extending from his toes to

the center of his skull. Someone who prided himself
on good health, Kissinger was initially unimpressed by
the impact of the flu, figuring a couple of aspirin
would knock it out of commission, and he had
shrugged off Brognola's suggestion that he cancel his
plans to drive up to Cape Cod for a long-anticipated
weekend of fishing and hunting. However, by the time
he'd driven out of Shenandoah National Park and had
started east on Interstate 211, the former pro line-
backer had found himself so weak and feverish that he
barely had the strength to get out of his car once he'd
stopped at the Happy Trails Inn.

After checking into a room, Kissinger had called the
Farm and made the necessary arrangements to get a
doctor sent out to make a house call at the motel. Told
that his best bet was to stay put and let the illness run
its course, Kissinger had promptly collapsed and fallen
asleep for the next eight hours, awakening to find that
Grimaldi and Brognola had stopped by to drop off the
medication, the VCR and a bag full of video movies.
He'd spent most of the past day and a half drinking
tea, sleeping, staring at the television and trying not to
think of how nice Cape Cod could be during the height
of spring bloom.

The kettle whistled and Kissinger took it off the
range, filling the pot and tossing in another bag of tea.
He sliced a lemon in half and squeezed its juice into a
cup, then took a small bite out of the bitter pulp, grimacing at the sour taste. He'd barely eaten since
checking into the room, and although his appetite was
returning he was still doubtful that he could hold
down food. Maybe by tomorrow, he hoped.

Kissinger poured tea into his cup and slumped back
into bed. He wasn't in the mood to watch any more

television. The phone was on the nightstand beside him and he put through a call to Stony Man Farm, making the usual screening precautions to ensure that he was on a clean line. Once he was cleared, Kissinger got Brognola on the second ring.

"'Lo, Chief."

"Cowboy? Is that you?"

"Doesn't feel like it, but yeah, it's me."

"Still down for the ten count?"

"Afraid so."

"Anything more we can get you?"

"A body transplant might be nice."

Brognola chuckled on the other end. "Good to hear you can at least make a joke about it. When we stopped by yesterday I thought for sure you were going to wind up in a straitjacket you were so frustrated."

"Well, I'm really not much better on that front," Kissinger confessed. "I just wanted to check in. How's the gang?"

"Well," Brognola began, "Jack's still here but Pol and Carl are down in Florida with Gadgets now." He went on to explain about the untimely death of Clark Meisner.

"Sorry to hear that," Kissinger said, stunned by the news. "Clark was a good man."

Kissinger had met Clark Meisner a few years back, when he was still working with the DEA. He'd had a short-lived relationship with Sandy at the time and on several occasions he'd run into her while in Florida. He remembered her brother fondly as a jovial, free-spirited man, full of stories and always in the midst of plans for some new, grand venture.

Kissinger sipped some tea as Brognola went on to describe how Able Team would be accompanying

Sandy when she went down to complete the ill-fated expedition. Brognola also mentioned Stephen Hokes and the Communist connection.

"Dammit, I wish I was going down there with them," Kissinger said.

"With your luck, you would have come down with jungle fever," Brognola told him. "Do yourself a favor and stay put."

"Speaking of jungle fever," Kissinger said, "what was the story on that dart that killed Meisner? It seems like they should have been able to pinpoint the poison and find an antidote, doesn't it?"

"We thought of that, too," Brognola said. "The coroner's going to be doing an autopsy tomorrow or the day after, depending on when they get caught up on all the other bodies piled up from all that street violence going on in our Sunshine state."

Kissinger drained his cup of tea, then told Brognola, "I tell you, Chief, somehow this whole thing just doesn't add up right for me."

"How so?"

"I'm not sure," Kissinger said, "but once I can shake this damn bug and get my wits about me, I want to check into it."

He wrapped up his call, then hung up the phone and stared absently at the ceiling. Dammit, what was it that he was trying to put his finger on? It felt to him as if the answer was lying just beyond his grasp, with the aches and fever of his illness holding him back from taking that one extra step needed to get a proper handle on things.

Reaching to his right, Kissinger snapped off the desk light, immersing the room in darkness. He crawled back beneath the covers and closed his eyes, letting his fatigue lull him back to sleep. He figured the sooner he rested up and shook this flu, the sooner he could get back to the real world.

7

Traffic was light on the Overseas Highway, a lengthy bridge linking Florida's Keys with the mainland. Tyne Murray sped along in her Mitsubishi Sigma, tape player blaring the sound track from *Woodstock*. Richie Havens was singing how sometimes he felt like a motherless child. Tyne thought back twenty years to when she was a college grad student who had passed up a chance to attend that legendary three-day concert because she had to cram for exams at NYC. She wasn't one for crowds and didn't want to hassle what was expected to be a turnout of thirty or forty thousand people. Of course, ten times as many concert-goers had shown up, but now she cursed herself for having missed out on what had become a high-water mark of the sixties.

So long ago. If she were able somehow to go back in time, she wondered if she'd even be able to recognize, much less understand the twenty-two-year-old Tyne Murray, whose major aspiration in life had been to be a social worker in the inner city, trying to single-handedly make the world a better place. Ah, but she was quite the specimen back then. White, liberal, naive, a woman poised on the crest of the feminist movement, ever the rebel with a cause.

"What a joke," she mused, taking one last drag of her cigarette and tossing it out the window.

During the years since Woodstock she'd had ample opportunity to shed her rose-colored glasses and see the world for what it really was, a magnificently brutal sprawl of conflicting ideals and cultures, filled with gray areas where the high-minded and self-righteous would inevitably find themselves run aground on the shoals of expediency. No one could thrive in such a world without first developing a flair for adaptability and a willingness to seize opportunities as they presented themselves.

Joan Baez was warbling about a drugstore truck drivin' man when Tyne pulled off the highway and took a side road to the far end of Fiddler Key, named after the crabs known to inhabit its sandy beaches. She turned off the radio and listened instead to the screeching of gulls gliding high on a coastal breeze sweeping in from the Gulf of Mexico. There was a distinct smell of brine and seaweed in the afternoon air, and as she drove into the parking lot for Shivering Timbers Wharf, she felt a pang of hunger at the mingling of these natural aromas with the unmistakable scent of fried oysters and conch fritters.

The wharf extended out on a long, dilapidated dock lined with bait shops, tourist eateries, souvenir stands and boat rental shacks. Gentle waves splashed against the barnacle-encrusted pilings below her as Tyne walked the weathered planks, ignoring the leering gazes of several old, ruddy-faced fishermen sitting in lawn chairs around a Styrofoam beer cooler near the pier railing.

"My, my," one of them crooned, giving Tyne the once-over. "Do I see a keeper here or what?"

"Might be," another chortled. "Wonder what kind of bait I'd need to reel her in."

Tyne shot the men a haughty glance.

"Oh, she's a fighter, she is," the oldest of the fisherman snickered. "Better get out the hundred pound test line."

"You're gonna need a better line than that," Tyne called out over her shoulder as she walked on. Her back turned to the men, she smiled to herself, secretly flattered by their attention. Having just passed that uneasy milestone of her fortieth birthday, it was reassuring to know that she could still turn a man's head with her looks. A well-meant leer a day made those two-hour exercise workouts worthwhile.

Toward the end of the pier, jutting out into the bay on an extension built next to the Shivering Timbers Bar and Grill, was a small, one-room shack, barely visible behind the tall wooden fence shielding it from the public. Tyne stopped before the locked gate and crouched down, swinging aside a hinged board that gave her access to a bell rope, to which she gave several quick tugs. Inside the compound, a rusty ship bell clanged noisily, scaring a pelican off the roof of the shack.

"Juan!" she called out, standing on tiptoe to peer above the top of the gate. "Jaisez! It's me, Tyne."

There was no answer from inside the shack, but next to it a monstrous ninety-pound rottweiler suddenly bolted out from its dog house, barking loudly as it charged the gate. Although she knew the dog was on a leash, Tyne still backed away reflexively. She'd been on hand several times when Jaisez had been putting the beast through attack training, and even now she could vividly picture the way the dog's slavering jaws snapped at the padded arms of its trainer.

"Shut up, Cortez!" she shouted over the dog's incessant yelping. "Where's your master?"

The dog continued to bark as it strained against its taut chain, which was connected to a guano-splattered post secured to the shack's foundation. Tyne waited a few moments longer, hoping the expedition guide would emerge from the shack. When there was still no sign of activity, she turned to leave just as a tall, pot-bellied man with tattooed arms and a chef's apron stepped out of the kitchen entrance to the bar and grill next door. He was carrying a cleaver and a handful of meat scraps.

"He ain't there," the man told Tyne when he recognized her.

"So I gathered," Tyne said. "Any idea when he'll be back?"

"Not apt to be for a while." The chef turned toward the shack, less than twenty feet away, and tossed the meat scraps over the fence. Cortez immediately fell silent and chased down the snacks. "Jaisez said something about going to see some family back north in Michigan. Told me to keep feeding the mutt for another week, ten days."

Tyne felt a flush of anger burn along her neck, but she did her best not to show it. Smiling at the chef, she said, "Well, I'll just have to wait and catch him when he gets back."

"No sense making this a wasted trip," the chef told her with a grin. "Come on in for some fritters and a few Rusty Nails. It's happy hour."

"Thanks, but I'm due somewhere," she said. "Another time, maybe."

"Yeah, yeah, that's what you always say," the big man sniffed. "You keep giving me the cold shoulder and I'm gonna break off our engagement."

Tyne laughed. "Please do."

Someone inside the bar was calling out for service, so the chef headed back inside and Tyne started for the parking lot. The smile fell away from her face and she ignored the good-natured taunts of the fishermen. Once she was back inside her Mitsubishi, she slammed her palm on the dashboard in anger.

"Michigan my ass," she spat. "I know where you went, you bastard Jaisez, and God help you when I catch up with you."

8

By midday the clouds broke over Skyler's Island, letting through the warm bronze glow of the sun. As they finished their lunch breaks, construction workers along the coast rolled up their sleeves, spreading layers of suntan lotion and insect repellent on their arms. The demolition crew signaled that they had concluded all their preparations, and a huge power crane moved slowly into position near the site of an old brick edifice that, half a century before, had anchored the island's once notorious penal colony. Long abandoned, the building's exterior was festooned with lichens and epiphytes, and its indoor cells and corridors had become the refuge of various forms of wildlife— from bright-colored macaws and toucans to brown coatis and white-headed capuchin monkeys. Smouldering fires had been set inside the building half an hour ago in hope that their billowing clouds of smoke would roust most of the creatures. But when three workers moved in with Springfield rifles and echoed several loud blasts off the inner walls, still more beasts took flight from the structure and headed for the nearby jungle.

"Okay!" the crew foreman finally called out, waving his arms to signal the crane operator.

Swinging its long, girdered neck away from the building, the crane built momentum for a huge wrecking ball suspended by a reinforced steel cable. As the crane reversed direction and guided the ball toward the building, the workers on the ground quickly scrambled back.

With a resounding crash the ball slammed into a section of outer wall. Aged brick and mortar rumbled down to the foundation, exposing a gaping hole.

"Few more swats like that and the whole thing'll be down," the foreman said happily as he surveyed the damage.

"Out with the old, in with the new, eh, boss?" the man beside him said, removing his hard hat long enough to wipe sweat off his forehead.

"Ain't that the truth."

Indeed, once the prison was demolished and the rubble was cleared away, a new foundation would be laid for the Coastline Sands, a multimillion-dollar hotel that would cater to a new clientele—those coming to Skyler's Island by choice rather than gunpoint. When completed in two years, the 833-room facility would be the cornerstone of a proposed resort complex extending along five miles of prime shorefront property. Three smaller hotels were being erected farther down the coast, and crews were laying connecting roads and plotting out thirty-six holes for a sprawling golf course that would reach into the jungle. Down at the southern tip of the island, an equally dramatic transformation was taking place as layers of fill were being compressed on an expanse of marshland that would eventually be converted into an airfield large enough to accommodate jumbo jets.

A consortium of backers, under the aegis of Coastal Sands Inc., had already put more than seventy-two million dollars into this project, envisioning the day when Skyler's Island would take its place alongside more-established resorts, such as Martinique and the Bahamas, as a getaway of choice for the upper classes and Club Med set.

The past few days, however, had seen a blow dealt to the relentless optimism that had thus far powered the project ahead of schedule. When people received word of the ambush that had befallen the Clark Meisner/Tyne Murray expedition, a pall of paranoia had settled upon both populated coasts of the island, fueled by daily rumors of widespread Doteine unrest and possible warfare among the other tribes of the interior. While there had been no further incidents to validate such rumors, the work crews had slowed their pace considerably, in part because there were always wary glances being cast toward the nearby jungle, and also because security details had been beefed up at the expense of the labor force.

Hoping to address the situation more effectively, Prime Minister Paray Mayos had agreed to a meeting with General Angel Timeli of the local militia and two resident supervisors of the resort project, Ed Redsana and Mickey Boldt. Mayos and Timeli had arrived shortly before noon from their palatial quarters on the opposite side of the island, accompanied by a twelve-man contingent of bodyguards.

The soldiers were now posted near the old penal colony, surrounding a sixty-foot-long house trailer serving as interim headquarters for the consortium. Inside, the trailer was lavishly appointed and linked to a pair of droning generators that provided adequate power to run the firm's computer and air-conditioning systems. The four men sat in a conference room dominated by a large model of the resort complex as it would look upon completion.

"Of course it would be unfortunate if you built all this and people were afraid to come visit," Mayos said, running a finger across the simulated asphalt of the proposed airfield. A corpulent, jowly man in his mid-fifties, the prime minister wore a gray silk suit with a diamond stickpin gleaming on his tie. He peered through thick-lensed spectacles at Redsana and Boldt. "None of us want this."

"None of us maybe, but the tribes are another matter," Redsana ventured. Roughly the same age as Mayos, Redsana was tall and gaunt, with an antiquated white beard divided into twin inverted pyramids. He pointed to the jungle interior as he returned Mayos's stare. A New Englander by birth, he still spoke with a faint Boston accent. "I needn't remind you that we had your assurance the natives wouldn't pose a threat to the resort."

"The ambush took place far from the coastline," Mayos reminded Redsana. "It was a case of their land being intruded upon."

"But when we secured a clearance for the expedition, our people were told the route was safe." Mickey Boldt, a balding, bulldog-faced man dressed in Banana Republic safari gear, rose from his chair as he spoke and opened the nearby refrigerator, taking out a bottle of chilled chardonnay. It had already been opened, and as he refilled the other men's glasses, he went on, "Now our men got it in their heads that any second we're gonna have Injuns on the beach looking for scalps."

Timeli, whose ancestry linked him to the tribes, gazed at Boldt with contempt. "Our people are not 'Injuns,'" the general intoned in flawless English. "And even the Doteine don't take scalps. You have been watching too many bad Hollywood movies."

"Don't duck the issue, General," Boldt countered. "We have a deal and you fucked up on your end."

Timeli sat upright, registering shock at the insolence of the Texan with the wine bottle. If any of his men so much as saluted him with less than the utmost of deference he could have their heads, and yet here he was forced to endure the tauntings of this boorish American. And why? Because by accident of birth Boldt had inherited a sizable fortune from his oilman father and parlayed it into an even larger fortune through fortuitous real estate investments and some less reputable dealings. And, of course, Timeli was also forced to indulge Boldt because a small but significant slice of the Texan's fortune and the fortunes of the whole consortium had been channeled to the general and prime minister as an inducement to gain their approval of the resort complex. A flat fee would make its way to the islanders' coffers during the construction phase; after that, Timeli and Mayos would theoretically be paid a percentage of all income derived by the completed facilities. It was therefore in the best interests of both natives to keep their people from doing anything that might put a damper of any future tourist trade.

"I've spoken to the tribe leaders," Timeli calmly told the Americans, "and they all claim no part in the ambush. Even the Doteine."

"Well," Redsana said, "that obviously can't be the case. But, whatever the explanation, something has to be done to put this issue to rest, once and for all."

The prime minister sipped his wine and eased back in his chair, reaching for a fig from a plate of fresh fruit set out on a serving table. As he peeled the skin back, he asked, "What do you propose?"

"A new deal," Redsana said. "One that will benefit all concerned."

Mayos and Timeli eyed one another skeptically. From the beginning, neither of them had placed much trust in the Americans, and for the most part their suspicions had been well placed. For example, the size and scope of the resort complex was now easily twice that which had initially been proposed, while the payoffs had not been increased proportionately. Instead, the consortium had begun to mix its payments with vague threats of extortion, hints that it might not set well with the tribes to discover how much their leaders were profiting from the development of the island. Mayos and Timeli had secretly discussed backing down on their commitments to the consortium and taking the enterprise under their sole control, but they knew that any such move would be self-defeating; it would scar the island's reputation even more than news of the ambush.

"We are listening," Mayos finally said, biting into the fig.

Redsana drew their attention to the model and pointed out different areas as he spoke. "Along here is a seven-mile-wide corridor of government land separating the tribes from the coast. At present, this land is untended and unguarded. As such, there is concern that any warring tribes could cross at any point and reach the resort area with minimal detection or resistance.''

"Not likely," Timeli said.

"But theoretically it's true," Redsana pushed on, "and it's a concern that must be addressed."

"What we propose is that the government land be sold to the consortium . . . for a price that you would find more than satisfactory."

"Out of the question!" the general snapped. "Absolutely not!"

"Look at the numbers before you jump the gun," Boldt advised. Opening a thin attaché case, the Texan removed a one-page contract and passed it over the model to Mayos and Timeli. "Here, count it up if you've got enough fingers."

The islanders perused the document carefully, with the prime minister resorting to a second pair of glasses to read the small print. The bottom line figures, however, were bold and underlined, impossible to miss and almost equally difficult to turn down. Lapsing into one of their native dialects, they whispered back and forth for several minutes while Redsana and Boldt calmly sipped their wine and peered out the trailer windows at the demolition of the penal institution.

"What are your plans for the land?" the prime minister finally asked.

"We just want it for a buffer, that's all," Redsana said. "We'll set up monitoring outposts to make sure tribes don't violate the borders, but other than that we'll leave the land untouched."

"If you will put that into writing and raise your price by a third, we will have deal."

"A third?" Boldt laughed. "What is this, Tijuana?"

Timeli said, "It takes some doing to change absolutely not into a yes."

"We'll flesh out the contracts and up the numbers thirteen percent," Redsana bartered, knowing full well that, unlike most Western cultures, on Skyler's Island the number thirteen was deemed a sign of good fortune.

"Take it or leave it," Boldt added.

Mayos and Timeli conferred briefly, then the prime minister extended a hand to Redsana. "We have a deal, gentlemen."

"Excellent," Redsana said, shaking Mayos's hand. "You'll be thanking yourself for years about this, believe me."

"If you say so," Mayos said.

A toast was proposed to the new agreement, and afterward the men finished off the last of the chardonnay. Then Mayos and Timeli rose from their chairs and bade the Americans good day. Stepping outside, they called out for their bodyguards to fall to attention, then barked out instructions for the trip back to the capital.

Back inside the trailer, Boldt returned to the refrigerator, pulling out yet another bottle of wine. He grinned at Redsana as he opened it. "Good job, Boston."

"It was a team effort," Redsana conceded. "We can both take credit."

"What about me?" Stephen Hokes said as he emerged from one of the back rooms of the trailer. "After all, the whole deal was my idea...."

ALTHOUGH THE PROPOSED AIRPORT was still well over a year from completion, there were two serviceable landing strips open to smaller craft like the Beech-craft Duke B60 Juan Jaisez was riding in. As the plane began its final descent out over the coastal waters, he could see workers laboring around the skeletal frame-work of the main terminal, as well as crews out laying asphalt on the new runway. Off in the distance a small motorcade forged its way along a narrow service road linking the resort development with the older native community on the far side of the island. Jaisez rec-ognized the prime minister's customized Cadillac El-dorado sandwiched between troop-filled pickups and guessed the reason for Mayos's visit.

"Good timing," he whispered under his breath.

"What's that?" pilot T. W. Glenn asked. He was a scrawny, freckle-faced redhead in his mid-twenties, with huge ears poking out either side of his narrow head.

"Nothing," Jaisez returned.

"You're sure I can land here with no problem?" Glenn asked, popping his bubble gum nervously as he pointed through the windshield. "I don't like the looks of that welcome wagon."

Down on the airfield, a jeep rolled into view and a man in back rose to a crouch, propping an Armbrust antitank weapon against his shoulder as he took aim at the Beechcraft.

"Fucking ay!" Jaisez quickly keyed the plane's ra-dio mike and cried out, "J. J. Tancoat, J. J. Tancoat. Do you read?"

For an insufferably long moment there was noth-ing but static crackling over the radio's small speaker, then a faint, disembodied voice finally droned, "Ro-ger, Tancoat. You're cleared for landing. Over."

"Gracias, Roberto," Jaisez replied. "Ten-four, over and out."

The jeep pulled off the runway and the man with the Armbrust lowered his weapon as the Duke B60 completed its descent and touched down evenly on the sun-bleached tarmac. On Jaisez's instructions, Glenn taxied over to a two-story structure of rusting corrugated steel that had served as the island's original hangar. By the time the plane had stopped and the two men inside had clambered down to the asphalt, the jeep had caught up with them. Jaisez flashed a grin at the driver, a baby-faced man whose swollen lips and twisted front teeth told of a penchant for fistfights.

"Hey, Roberto, what it is?"

Roberto traded high fives with Jaisez and told him, "You guys snuck in just in time."

"What do you mean?" Jaisez wondered.

"Storm blowing in later on," Roberto said, pointing out toward the distant Atlantic, where an ominous bank of dark clouds could be seen gathering along the horizon.

Jaisez shrugged. "Forget the storm, I was more worried about the thunder your boyfriend's packing," he muttered, gesturing behind Roberto at the man with the Armbrust, a middle-aged Irishman with a hawk nose and shock-white hair flowing beneath a Boston Red Sox baseball cap. "Hey, Johnny, where'd you get that oversized pecker, anyway?"

"Two pair high." Johnny laughed, slapping the side of the weapon. "Bluffed Marty a good one."

"Well, if you guys are up for another game," Jaisez told the men in the jeep, "T.W. here plays a fair game of stud. Best poker face in the Keys."

T.W. nodded greetings to Roberto and Johnny. "Juan is exaggerating a little."

"Well, we'll just have to find out, won't we?" Roberto said as he got out of the jeep, followed by Johnny.

"While you guys get into it, how about if I borrow the wheels?" Jaisez suggested. "I need to talk to the honchos."

Roberto handed him the keys and gave him a light pat on the cheek. "Drive safely," he joked, "and don't be home late."

"*Si, papa.*"

As the other men headed into the old hangar, Jaisez started up the jeep and drove past the construction crews. He briefly deliberated trying to catch up with the prime minister, but decided that he didn't know Mayos well enough to do the kind of hard bargaining he had in mind. Besides, he figured that his position would be stronger with the Cartel. He could get them to cut a sweet enough deal to make things worth his while, and with any luck he'd get to them ahead of Tyne.

Heading north, he passed the various construction projects, marveling at the fast pace of the building. It had to take a lot of money to get a sprawl this big off the ground, and Jaisez felt that he was entitled to a bit more of that money than what he'd been given for his small role in helping to set up the ambush of Clark Meisner's expedition.

"A *lot* more money," he murmured over the jeep's drone.

It took him fourteen minutes to negotiate his way along the half-built roadways to the demolished penal colony and the house trailer Redsana and Boldt ran the development out of. When Redsana answered his knock with a surprised expression on his face, Jaisez walked past him, grinning, and waved nonchalantly at Boldt and Stephen Hokes.

"Buenos dias, gringos," he called out happily. "How about a little vino for your new partner?"

9

In recent years, the Drug Enforcement Agency's overseas activity had increased incrementally with the corresponding growth of drug trafficking around the globe. In most cases their foreign input consisted primarily of providing training and technological support to local antidrug units like the Leopards of Bolivia and Peru's Sweepsquads. But there were also instances when the DEA sought a more hands-on involvement with some foreign enemy, especially if they suspected corruption among local officials. In those cases, the call went out to a small, elite cadre of seasoned veterans who had subjected themselves to a rigorous training rivaling that given to the Green Berets, Navy SEALS and other U.S. Special Forces, including Able Team.

"This is quite the playground," Gadgets Schwarz said after Sandy had given the Team a tour through the DEA's special-agent training grounds, an isolated, eighty-acre parcel of land in the Everglades located eleven miles inland from Miami. Like some strange aberration of the benign theme attractions of Orlando's Disney World, the compound was divided into separate areas, each one simulating the environment of various drug-harvesting centers around the world, from South America's hilly cocaine plots to the sprawling opium fields of the Far East.

"It is, isn't it?" Sandy agreed, glancing at the dense jungle growth surrounding them. "And it's pretty realistic, too, don't you think?"

Lyons nodded as he tugged on a hanging vine suspended from a tree behind him. "Yeah. I half expected Tarzan to come swinging by any minute."

"Kinda reminds me of Nam. Jungle Warfare School," Blancanales reflected. He ran a finger through his thinning hair and quickly added, "Of course, that was a couple years back."

"Just a couple," Schwarz said. "We're so much more...experienced now."

"That's the word I was looking for." Pol unsheathed the machete he'd been given and made a few swipes through the air. "Well, I've got calluses in all the right places, so at least I won't have blisters to worry about."

"No, but you might want to get in a few hours of hacking at underbrush," Sandy advised. "You'd be surprised how fast your wrists can give out."

"I'll take your word for it," Pol said, pointing off to his left. "That looks like a good place to start. I'll see you guys in a while...unless you hear me doing my Johnny Weissmuller impression, in which case I'll probably be sinking fast in one of the sand pits."

"I want to get in a little practice on the river crossings," Lyons said.

"We'll do some stalking," Schwarz said, including Sandy in the activity. "We can all meet back here in, say, an hour."

"Fair enough," Blancanales said, heading off.

Lyons broke away from the others, lengthening his stride as he made his way along a barely discernible trail. Forty yards later he was lost in the overgrowth and had to resort to his machete to make further progress. Between slashes, he listened intently, trying to pinpoint the sound of running water. After more than twenty minutes of hard negotiating, he finally cleared his way to the bank of a wide watercourse running through the middle of the training ground. Twenty-five yards across, the tributary ran deep and turbulent, much the way the Aitacon River flowed into the heart of Skyler's Island. Although the DEA hadn't gone to the extent of stocking the river with caiman and piranhas to duplicate the dangers of the tropical waters, it was common knowledge that alligators lurked about the compound, having made a remarkable comeback from the endangered-species list. As such, Lyons wasn't about to attempt the most expedient way of crossing the river, which would have been to drop into the water and swim against the current until reaching the other side. Instead he scanned the banks until he spotted a crude makeshift bridge of hemp and vines drawn tautly from one embankment to the other. There were only three strands, one meant for walking on and the other two for handholds.

Lyons made his way to where the bridge began. Pausing to catch his breath, he noticed that his forearm was bleeding from where he'd brushed against a razor-edged blade of saw grass. It was only a superficial wound, but he knew that such a scrape would be of concern on Skyler's Island, where the risk of infection would be greater, not to mention that even the faintest trace of blood could draw the attention of jungle predators, be they land-bound panthers or the carnivores of the deep.

"Shit," Lyons grumbled, pulling a bandanna from his back pocket and dabbing at his arm until the bleeding stopped. Then, stepping out onto the thickest vine, he steadied himself and began to inch forward. The vine sagged considerably under his two hundred pounds and his muscles tensed as he fought for balance with each tenuous step, clutching the two higher vines for support. It had been some time since he'd gone through such a maneuver, and he was surprised that something so simple looking could be so difficult. Of course, the fact that natives traversed such bridges barefoot instead of wearing thick-soled insulated boots had something to do with it, and halfway across Lyons was wondering if it hadn't been a mistake not to follow their example. But there was no turning back at this point.

Inch by inch, Lyons continued, hearing the current run beneath him, frothing where water splashed over rocks and snags. Loud and distracting as the rapids were, Lyons was still attuned enough to other noises around him, particularly the sound of someone approaching the opposite bank. Tightening his left hand on the support vine, Lyons balanced himself precariously and glanced up.

Tyne Murray was standing at the end of the bridge, holding a machete aloft as if she intended to sever the vines that supported Lyons.

"The natives decide they don't want you around," she said. "What do you do?"

"Depends," Lyons said, thinking quickly. "Anyone with you?"

"Two archers," she said. "One on either side of me."

"Aiming at me?"

"Yes."

"Well . . . not much choice."

Lyons suddenly changed position, crouching low on the span and leaning his weight against his left arm, which he curled around the support vine to give him better balance. His right hand went to his shoulder holster, coming out with a Colt .45 Government Model. Set in semiautomatic mode, the weapon barked three times in quick succession, burying slugs into the tree to Tyne's left. A split second later, Lyons fired two shots into another tree just to the woman's right, then leveled the weapon at Tyne, grinning savagely.

"Five shots left," he told her.

Tyne inspected the two trees and cocked an appreciative eyebrow as she lowered her machete. "I think the native is impressed and makes a strategic retreat, but fast."

Lyons holstered his .45 and stood up, then cleared the distance to the far embankment. Tyne stepped aside as he planted his feet back on solid ground.

"Very impressive, I must say," she told him.

"Actually, if it was crunch time I would have had to sweep the bank and take you out with the others," Lyons said, rubbing his forearm where the vine had chafed his skin.

"Lucky for me it was only a test, then."

He eyed Tyne curiously. "So tell me, what's a nice girl like you doing in a place like this?"

"Your aim's better than your wit," she said, laughing.

"Stands to reason," Lyons said. "Hard to bring down the bad guys with a punch line."

"I suppose so." Tyne sheathed her machete. "I checked with DEA and found out you guys were out here. I wanted to come by and apologize for playing devil's advocate after the memorial service."

"No harm, no foul," Lyons said with a shrug.

"Truth is," she went on, "I've given it some thought and, if it's okay with all of you, I'd like to string along when you go down there."

"Now that *is* a change of heart," Lyons said.

"Well, I understand Sandy's position, and I just don't feel right about turning my back on anything that might ensure that her brother didn't die in vain." The woman turned solemn for a moment. "I mean, I was right next to him when he took that dart. It could have been me."

"All the more reason not to want to go back."

"What's that supposed to mean?" Tyne snapped with sudden anger. "I'm not a coward, damn you."

"Whoa, take it easy," Lyons said. "That's not what I meant."

"The hell it wasn't."

"Look, let's not get bogged down in this, okay? If you want to come along, it seems like a good enough idea to me. You know the area and the political situation down there. It'd be a big help. Can you still get clearance, being retired and all?"

Tyne nodded. "I don't think I really need it for just the expedition, but I'm sure it would be no problem. I can even put you in touch with some Company people on the island. Who knows, maybe they have some stuff on Hokes I'm not privy to."

Lyons checked his weatherproof watch. "Well, I'm due back shortly. Why don't you tag along and we'll check with the others."

"Good idea."

Lyons stepped to one side and bowed at the waist as he gestured to the bridge. "Ladies before gentlemen."

Tyne laughed. "My, so debonair. Maybe I should have worn an evening gown."

"I might like to see that sometime," Lyons confessed.

Tyne cast a coquettish glance back at Lyons. "And I think you'd be an eyeful in a sport coat."

"Why don't we find out?" Lyons suggested. "We aren't leaving until morning. We could have dinner tonight."

Tyne smiled. "You're on, Mr. Lyons."

Stepping out on the vine ladder, she guided herself along the tight span with dazzling grace. Lyons watched her with admiration. Somewhere in the back of his mind it occurred to him that he hadn't really been involved with a woman since the death of his beloved Julie Harris more than two years ago. Staring at Tyne, he couldn't help but wonder if perhaps he was at long last through mourning.

10

Juan Jaisez rode contentedly in the back seat of Stephen Hokes's diesel Jetta, watching macaws take flight into the surrounding jungle as they pushed along the two-lane vein of blacktop that ran from the coast to Hokes's remote plantation. He was glad he'd summoned the courage to bluff his hand with Hokes and the others because he sensed that they respected his audacity. They were cutting him in on the action as much out of respect as concern that he might indeed blow the whistle on the hidden agenda behind their development of the island.

"So, Juan," Redsana asked him, glancing over the backrest of the front seat. "Just out of curiosity, how did you piece all this information together?"

Jaisez smiled slyly. "I've met my share of people over the years. I have connections. When I first became suspicious, I knew who to put the right questions to. Sometimes that's all it takes."

"Ain't that the truth," Mickey Boldt sniggered, jabbing an imported Panama cigar between his teeth and lighting it. He was sitting beside Jaisez and offered the guide another of the cigars. Jaisez helped himself and puffed smoke rings as the Texan blathered on. "And somebody with those kinda connections can be a big help to us. Hell, you should've come to us sooner, y'know? Would have saved the trouble of that little scene we had back at the trailer.''

Jaisez smiled smugly as he recalled the look on the men's faces when he told them he'd compiled an extensive dossier of Coastal Sands Inc.'s various surreptitious activities based out of Skyler's Island. He knew about the ambush of Clark Meisner, the harboring of Hokes, the coke smuggling scheme and even tentative plans to create a guerrilla training base inside the jungle interior. He said the file was in the hands of friends back in Florida, friends who would mail the information to federal authorities if they didn't hear from Jaisez by the end of the following day. That revelation had begun a brief bartering session, during which Jaisez had laid out the terms by which he would agree to sit on the information he'd gathered. Hokes and the others had bargained as hard as circumstances would allow, but in the end they had buckled under and cut a deal to Jaisez's satisfaction.

Fifteen percent off the top of any undocumented income; nine percent of all other monies. A tidy sum indeed.

And, in all fairness, Jaisez made sure that the arrangement wasn't totally one-sided. No mere extortionist, he also volunteered to put something back into the Cartel's kitty. Specifically, he would not only abide by a promise to hold his tongue about all illegal activity, but he would also put his network of connections to use in arranging for the smuggling of cocaine not only into the United States but also into the more lucrative European market. All in all, it had been agreed by the others that the addition of Jaisez to their midst could prove, in the long run, to be a boon to their business. Hokes had gone so far as to say that if Jaisez played square and proved his worth down the line, the numbers of their agreement would be renegotiated in his favor. That had been the icing on the cake.

"What's important," Jaisez told Boldt between puffs on his cigar, "is that we all understand and respect one another. Given that, what's a little squabbling among friends?"

"He's right," Hokes said as he guided the Jetta around one last bend and burst through the blanketed canopy of jungle to a clearing fenced off by a wall of spike-topped wrought-iron bars that allowed for a partial glimpse of the plantation grounds. While he waited for the huge main gate to be opened by security guards, Hokes looked over at the other men. "I think we should look on today as a real breakthrough. For all of us."

"Oh, I agree," Redsana said. "Absolutely."

"Ditto," Boldt said.

Jaisez grinned and gave the group a thumbs-up gesture. "Amen."

Pulling onto plantation property, Hokes headed down the lengthy driveway, veering right at a fork that took the men to the processing plant, a nondescript cinder-block building half-hidden from view behind a row of closely spaced trees.

"Give Juan a look at what we're up to," Hokes said as he idled the Jetta near the plant entrance. "I have some business to attend to at the mansion for a couple of hours, but I'll have the chef whip up a real feast for tonight so we can celebrate in style."

"Sounds good to me," Jaisez said as he got out of the car.

"Do you enjoy female company?" Hokes asked him.

Jaisez countered, "Does a thirsty man like water?"

Hokes smiled. "Consider it done."

As Hokes drove off toward the mansion, Jaisez took one last puff on his cigar, then cast it aside and beamed at Boldt and Redsana. "I think I'm going to like this...."

IT WAS LATE in the afternoon when Bernardo Octria and four of his fellow Colombians returned from the fields, where they'd spent the day watching slaves draw latex from the rubber trees and transfer it into twenty-five gallon, stainless-steel containers. The containers had been loaded onto four separate wooden carts, each drawn by three yoke-bound, domesticated koupreys. The ring-eyed oxen were boarded in a large pen adjacent to the processing plant, and while the other Colombians untethered the beasts and led them to the feeding troughs, Octria held his Smith & Wesson in clear view and watched carefully as the fatigued Thiglada tribesmen formed a line and began passing the heavy canisters of latex down from the carts and over to the main entrance of the processing plant. It was a tedious task, and Octria's men returned from the pens well before it had been completed. Octria left them to watch the slaves and entered the plant, which reeked of a sickly sweet, pungent odor attributable to the latex and the various forms of acid used to coagulate it into loaf-sized blocks of raw rubber, which would later be bundled into loads for shipment overseas.

For the past quarter century, petroleum-based synthetic rubbers had far outstripped their natural counterparts in terms of production, but there was still sufficient room in the marketplace for the latter. The

Hokes plantation turned out sufficient quantities to serve as a front for the far greater profits earned through less toutable enterprises.

The plant was run by a carefully chosen crew of trained tribesmen who had proven themselves trustworthy and dedicated during earlier stints as field hands. Their loyalty was imperative, as they oversaw a critical link in the Cartel's smuggling operations. Octria lingered near one of the tall, triangular racks where semisolid sheets of latex from the acid tanks were passed through rollers that squeezed out excess moisture and readied them for a final trip through drying tunnels. Before this last step, however, the sheets of rubber were set into a specially designed mold, where they would thickly encase a core of either refined cocaine or wads of thick cocaine paste that would later be turned into crack. After months of testing, Hokes's people had come across an additive that, when mixed with the curing acids, would mask any trace of the cocaine if the loads should undergo cursory inspections by canine units used by the DEA and Customs officials to detect the presence of drugs in cargo shipments.

Octria watched as a clot of cocaine paste was squeezed and sealed into a plastic tube before being set in the mold. Once in position, the tube vanished from view and a sheet of rubber was mechanically drawn into the mold. There was a hissing of pistons compressing the parcel into shape, then the mold unhinged and the completed brick was pulled out by a worker and set into a rack already half-filled with similar loads destined for the drying tunnel. This was quite a change from the way things were done in Octria's native Colombia, where peasants created their crude balls of paste by dumping coca leaves and chemicals into large outdoor pits, then hauled the sticky, soiled wads to makeshift marketplaces for sale to eager buyers from one of the cartels. Here the paste was concocted on the other side of the main chamber in large stainless-steel cauldrons, cutting down on waste and increasing the overall efficiency of the processing and ensuring a greater potency when the paste was transformed into crack.

Octria glanced up from the assembly-line production after a few minutes and did a double-take when he saw Juan Jaisez standing with Ed Redsana and Mickey Boldt on the other side of the plant.

"What the fuck?" he cursed under his breath, breaking away from the processing racks. Before he could cross the room, however, Octria felt a hand on his shoulder and turned around to see Stephen Hokes.

"Hold it," Hokes said softly.

"What's Jaisez doing here?" Octria asked, anger in his voice. "I told you last week what he did back in Colombia during the raids. I thought you said you believed me and—"

"Shh," Hokes told him. "I still believe you, Bernardo. It's being taken care of."

"Then why is he here with—"

"It's being taken care of," Hokes interrupted. "Now, get out of here before he sees you. If you want, you can go out by the nests and wait. We'll be bringing him by there shortly."

"The nests?" Octria's face slowly changed expression, his anger giving way to a look of approval. "This should be something to see."

Hokes nodded. "Yes. Now go."

Octria shot one last glance at Jaisez, then silently slipped out the side door. He couldn't wait to get to the nests.

JUAN JAISEZ RODE in front as Hokes drove his Jetta off the plantation grounds and down a dirt path leading into the island's government-protected wilderness preserve.

"This will be perfect for our needs," Redsana said as he looked around at the surrounding jungle. "There should be plenty of suitable places to plant coca."

"And to set up a base for our friends," Boldt added. "We'll see a few pretty pennies off that, too."

"Money from Moscow?" Jaisez wondered.

"Who cares where it comes from," Boldt wisecracked. "Long as there's enough of it and it's negotiable, it could be coming from the damn Martians for all I care."

The four men shared a laugh as Hokes drove farther and farther into the green depths of the interior. Jaisez spied a few spider monkeys swinging through the upper reaches and marveled at their effortless dexterity. "How far away is this place?" he finally asked.

"Not much farther," Hokes assured him.

Jaisez rubbed his hands together and grinned back at the men seated behind him. "I can't wait to see these ladies after all you've told me."

"Oh, you'll do more than see them," Boldt promised. "I'm telling you, you never had it like this."

Half an hour later Hokes pulled off what passed for the main road and guided the Jetta down twin dirt ruts leading through a bank of thorny bushes to the first clearing they'd seen since leaving the plantation. The sudden brightness of the unobstructed sun blinded Jaisez for a moment and he screened his eyes with the back of his hand. He blinked several times, and as his vision returned he felt the unmistakable cold touch of a gun barrel pressing against the back of his neck.

"We're here, Jaisez," Boldt whispered menacingly in his ear. "Time for your big surprise."

As Jaisez's eyes adjusted to the light, he glanced out the windshield and saw that the clearing was filled with tall, conical mounds of dirt, some as high as a man. He'd been on enough expeditions in his life to know the source of the mounds. A sick feeling suddenly rolled through him.

"No," he murmured.

Hokes reached over and frisked Jaisez, removing the man's automatic pistol. "You won't be needing this, Juan."

Boldt continued to hold a small .22 against Jaisez's neck as Redsana got out of the Jetta and opened the side door. "Out," he told Jaisez, backing up the command by revealing a Weatherby Mark V rifle he'd taken from the rear trunk. A bolt-action .460 Magnum, the Mark V contained 500-grain bullets with an unsurpassed firing velocity and more than enough impact force to bring down any form of game. Jaisez knew that he'd have a better chance of surviving a sledgehammer to the skull than a direct hit from the Weatherby.

Weak in the knees, he warily slid out of the car and joined Redsana in the clearing. "There's been some kind of mistake," he protested feebly.

"Yes, and we plan to rectify that," Redsana told him.

Boldt and Hokes joined Redsana and led Jaisez toward the dirt mounds, pinning his arms behind his back. He staggered under their insistent prodding, almost losing his balance. Finally Boldt reached out and shoved the man to the ground. Redsana took aim with the Weatherby and fired one shot, which reverberated loudly across the clearing and into the jungle. Jaisez grimaced in agony, clutching at the bloody mess of shattered tendon and cartilage that had once been his right knee. Tears of pain welled in his eyes and he shouted at his tormentors, "Kill me and you'll be exposed! Ruined!"

"Oh, is that a fact?" Hokes said calmly. "And who's going to expose us? Your friends Dennis Burks and Roger Cravens?"

Jaisez tried not to betray his shock at the mention of the two men's names, but there was no point in the facade.

"They've already been taken care of," Hokes told him. "I don't think they'll be mailing anything to the authorities."

Redsana fired the Mark V and took out Jaisez's other kneecap, reducing the once haughty schemer to a crippled, whimpering beggar. "Stop!" he wailed. "Or kill me and be done with it!"

"I think not," Redsana told him. "Not after what you've done."

"It was bad enough that you had to concoct this little blackmail enterprise of yours, Jaisez," Boldt said. "But we also found out that back when you were in South America, you made a little money by leading the *federales* to some of our people's drug haunts."

"Not true!" Jaisez cried. "I never did that! I was only a guide to private expeditions. I didn't work for the government."

"Liar!" Bernardo Octria shouted as he stepped into view at the edge of the clearing. "You helped to break the Cartel by giving information to *federales*."

"No!"

"Yes!" Octria maintained as he strode toward the fallen guide. "You told them you wanted to be anonymous, but some secrets are not meant to be kept. You helped them and they broke up the heart of our ring. They killed my brother the same day you were back in Florida taking money from Meisner to help guide his expedition here!"

In a fit of rage, Octria lashed out with his steel-tipped boots, kicking Jaisez with so much force that the snapping of ribs was heard above the victim's impassioned screams.

"Cry all you want, Jaisez!" Octria taunted between kicks. "No one will hear you except the ants!"

When he was finished beating Jaisez, Octria single-handedly dragged the man into the midst of the conical mounds, then cast him headfirst into the sand. Before Jaisez could react, Octria lashed out with his feet again, kicking the guide in the back until the man's spine had been traumatized to the point where he could no longer move. Then he spat at Jaisez and took a step back, reaching into his khaki jacket. Withdrawing a half-pint jar of honey, Octria unscrewed the lid and poured its contents over Jaisez's head. The wounded man gagged slightly as the substance trailed down his face and into his nose and mouth. He had to blink to keep it from his eyes, and even that slight effort required the utmost of concentration.

Taking a broken bough from a nearby tree, Octria clutched it like a club and took a full swing at the mound closest to Jaisez. The top of the cone crumbled under the force of the blow and soon a fierce stream of large red ants began pouring out of the nest, descending like a flow of lava toward the immobile form of the wounded man.

"You'll find that they tickle a little bit, yes?" Octria chuckled as he backed away from the nest.

Jaisez screamed anew with an almost inhuman intensity as the small creatures swarmed across him, attacking him with their small, razorlike pincers and following the sweet flow of honey into his nose and mouth. In a matter of mere seconds it was difficult to see the man for all the ants that blanketed him, and by the time Octria had rejoined the others, Jaisez's screams had been strangled by the choking volume of insects crawling down his throat.

To Octria's surprise, he saw that Boldt had a small hand-held video camera in his hands and was recording the grisly execution. "It'll make a great motivational tape for anyone who might think about crossing us in the future." The Texan chuckled as he zoomed in on the barely recognizable body of the late Juan Jaisez.

Redsana smiled thinly as he took the Weatherby back to the Jetta and returned it to the trunk. "I don't think I'll be pouring honey on my pancakes for a while."

11

"I don't know if this is a good idea," Jack Grimaldi told John Kissinger as they slipped into a rental car at Miami International Airport. "Damn, Cowboy, you still look like death warmed over."

"I don't feel much better than I look," Kissinger confessed, "but I had to get down here and look into a few things."

"We already missed the Team," Grimaldi said, glancing at his watch. "They headed out for Skyler's Island an hour ago."

"That's okay," Kissinger said. "Even I'm not stubborn enough to think I could hold my own on some jungle trek."

"That's a relief," Grimaldi muttered, paying a parking attendant and driving out onto Le Jeune Road. It was midafternoon and they were promptly bogged down by the first onslaught of rush-hour traffic.

Kissinger still felt a dull ache throughout his body and his head was less than clear, but he was grateful to be out of the motel room and back among the living. The more thought he'd given to the death of Clark Meisner, the less satisfied he was with the official explanation of the circumstances surrounding the ambush on Skyler's Island. It had taken some cajoling and arm-twisting, but he'd finally convinced Grimaldi to accompany him to Miami, where he planned to gather all the pertinent facts and find a way to make them add up to the truth.

Their first stop was at the county morgue, but by the time they'd shown up, the coroner was gone for the day and no one else was either willing or able to provide them with any conclusive information on the results of Meisner's autopsy. They would release only the fact that his death had been officially attributed to poison-related heart failure.

"Dammit!" Kissinger snapped impatiently as they left the building. "Why'd that guy have to pick today of all days to leave town without a forwarding number?"

"Easy, Cowboy," Grimaldi told him. "He'll be back tomorrow, okay? Come on, we can still check out the zoo folks, then turn in early. It'll be morning before you know it."

"Yeah," Kissinger said as he got back in the car. "It's just one of those things where you feel like you're racing against the clock, y'know?"

"Not really." Grimaldi drove back out into traffic, making his way for the South Dixie Highway. "I mean, no offense, but the guy's already dead," he told Cowboy. "It's not like you're going to be able to save him somehow."

"I know that," Kissinger admitted. "That's not what I'm getting at. I just can't believe that things happened the way that they were explained to me. Clark was a pro. He knew what he was doing and it doesn't track that he'd run up against some hostile tribe just to take photos of some mystery cows."

"The way I heard it, he thought he was in safe country and by all accounts this Doteine tribe wasn't supposed to be within a dozen miles of his expedition route," Grimaldi said. "Who could have known they'd be pushing past their borders? It was a fluke, that's all."

Kissinger shook his head. "Too much of a coincidence if you ask me. I just don't buy it."

"Then what do you think? That these Doteine had spies who got word about the expedition and sent out a hit squad to nail Meisner because they didn't want the world to know they've cornered the market on spectacled kouprey? Get real, Cowboy. That fever's scrambled your brains a little, if you ask me."

"Look, just trust me on this, would you?" Kissinger countered.

"Fine," Grimaldi said with a shrug. "Just don't start laying any psychic babble on me about intuition or whatever. I get enough of that from Schwarz."

It was closing time at Metrozoo when they finally showed up, but fortunately they were better received than at the morgue and they quickly found themselves ushered into the office of Gardner Richwell, the man who'd delivered Meisner's eulogy at the memorial service. Richwell listened earnestly as Kissinger laid out his misgivings about the official story concerning Meisner's death, nodding his head several times.

"As a matter of fact," he said after Kissinger had finished, "I'm also perplexed about things. If it's any consolation to you, your associates spoke to me before leaving for Skyler's Island this afternoon, and Mr. Lyons said he planned to look into the situation when they arrived there."

"Well, that's a little bit of a relief," Kissinger said, casting a look at Grimaldi. "I was beginning to feel like Don Quixote here."

"Do you have some sort of theory about this?" Richwell asked Cowboy.

"Not really," Kissinger said. "Clark stepped on his share of toes over the years, so it could be that somebody had it in for him."

"Perhaps," Richwell said. "I know a handful of enemies he'd made the past couple of years. You'd be surprised how much politics goes into this adventuring business, not to mention the search for endangered species."

"But if someone wanted to get him, why go to all the trouble of setting up something in the middle of some godforsaken jungle?" Grimaldi wondered. "There are a lot easier and less complicated ways to off somebody."

Richwell swiveled in his plush leather chair and idly spun a mounted globe sitting on the edge of his desk. "It's a very big world out there, Mr. Grimaldi. Some of the stories our people bring back from the field are simply amazing."

"I'm sure, but let's get off this tangent for a second. What can you tell us about the people who helped finance the expedition? Some kind of consortium putting up hotels or something down on the beaches there?" the Stony Man pilot asked.

Richwell nodded. "Coastal Sands. We did a check on them. They're legitimate and the terms of our collaboration were more than satisfactory. Naturally there was some sort of tax maneuvering behind their helping to underwrite the expedition, but pure altruism would probably have been even more suspect in this day and age. And good heavens, Tyne Murray worked for our intelligence people all those years, after all. If you can't trust someone like that, then who can you?"

"Good point," Kissinger said. "Listen, maybe it'd be worthwhile if I talked with her about all this. Do you know where I can reach her?"

Richwell smiled ironically. "You don't know?"

"Know what?"

"Why, she's with your friends, on her way back to the island."

"You're kidding."

"No, no. On the contrary." Richwell gently rubbed the edge of his fingernail across his mustache, as if sorting the hairs into place. "I think she somehow wants to make amends for what happened to Meisner. At least that's the impression she gave to me."

"Damn, this just isn't my day," Kissinger groaned.

Grimaldi was looking over the photographs of various acquisitional expeditions for some of the exotic animals now living on Metrozoo's spacious grounds. On a hunch, Grimaldi asked the older man, "Would you by any chance have the names of some of the other people in Meisner's party? Besides Murray?"

"Well, now, most of the party was made up of local tribesmen," Richwell said. "Roiyads. Easily the most peaceful of all the natives, and the most fit for trailblazing."

"But wasn't there anyone else?" Grimaldi pressed. "Somebody who might be here in the States? An interpreter or something?"

"As a matter of fact . . ." Richwell sat forward and gave his desk a quick, deft pat, then leaned forward and sorted through his out file until he found a manila envelope. He pulled out a twenty-six-page document filled with requisition forms and other paperwork dealing with the ill-fated expedition. As he began flipping through pages, he said, "There *was* a guide that Clark and Murray hired on. Short fellow with a lot of credits to his name. He was very determined to get the assignment and, as his luck would have it, the man who was supposed to lead the way came down with a terrible case of food poisoning and had to bow out. Ah, here it is...."

Richwell folded back the other pages and handed the file document to Kissinger. Grimaldi looked over Cowboy's shoulder at Juan Jaisez's background application and a letter of recommendation from the editor of a prestigious national magazine devoted to overseas exploration.

"Guy sounds like a regular jungle rat," Grimaldi said, skimming the document.

"Has an address down in the Keys, too," Kissinger said with a hint of expectation. "No phone number, but I think we're about due for a break, don't you?"

"Yep," Grimaldi said, grabbing a pad and pen from Richwell's desk and jotting down Jaisez's address. "And, who knows, if traffic clears up a little, we might even get there by sundown."

"Or at least dinnertime," Kissinger said, handing the document back to Richwell. "Thanks for the help."

"I hope it works out for you."

"Join the club," Kissinger said.

12

Tyne Murray looked out at the patchy clouds below her, then turned from the plane's window and smiled at Carl Lyons.

"Yes?" Lyons asked.

"I was just thinking about dinner last night," she said. "That story about you cornering the possum when you were on the police force."

"It happened just the way I told it," Lyons vowed, placing his hand over his chest. "Scout's honor."

"I believe you," she said, breaking into a light laugh. "I can just picture your face when you opened that door and found it staring up at you from inside the toilet bowl...and you trying to flush it before it could get out. Yech."

"Okay, so I'm not a big-game hunter," Lyons said with a blush. He put a finger to his lips and gestured for Tyne to keep her voice down so the others couldn't hear them. "Let's not ruin my reputation over it, okay?"

"Okay, okay," Tyne said, glancing across the cabin.

Schwarz and Sandy were sitting across from them inside the eight-seater Corsair jet they'd secured through Hal Brognola's influence with the Coast Guard. Blancanales was up front in the cockpit, conferring with the pilot as he glanced over topo maps of Skyler's Island.

Tyne leaned back in her seat, stifling a yawn before asking Lyons, "And it was after the possum incident that you decided to get out of police work and into something safer, right?"

"Hardly," Lyons scoffed. He told her about his transfer to the LAPD's organized-crime strike force, a stint that earned him the notice of the Justice Department. Although such details about his life were normally buried beneath a cover story intended to protect the confidentiality of Lyons's later involvement with Able Team, in this case he felt no need to pull his punches. If anything, the truth somehow came easy for him when he was with Tyne, as their dinner the previous evening had proven. They'd ended up at their table for more than four hours, putting away two bottles of an expensive burgundy as they'd talked the night away. He found himself attracted to her straightforward manner and the clear intensity of her dark eyes. There was also something about the faint, alluring scent of her glossy hair that aroused him. It had taken a firm resolve not to push for a more intimate end to the evening, and even then he'd found it difficult to get to sleep once he was back at the hotel suite where Blancanales and Schwarz had already dozed off. And now the attraction was still there, nagging at him, making their proximity in the plane a near-maddening exercise in self-restraint. Come on, Ironman, he chided himself at one point, you're acting like you're back in high school.

Tyne chuckled impishly when he'd finished. "All that cloak-and-dagger work. I bet you must have met your share of beautiful women, yes?"

Lyons stiffened at the remark, caught off guard by the rush of buried emotions it unearthed. Beautiful women? Yeah, he'd met his share, from Flo Trujillo to Margaret Williams to Julie Harris...each of them radiantly unique and beguiling, offering him a challenging and rewarding relationship. Each of them now but a memory, taken from him by the Reaper.

"I'm sorry," Tyne said, sensing Lyons's discomfort. "I didn't mean to upset you."

"That's okay," he said. After a beat, he added, eyes focused on the great blue beyond, "There have been a few women, but they...they all were cut down by the scum out there."

"I'm sorry," Tyne repeated, instinctively placing her hand on his forearm. "I should have known..."

"No, you couldn't have."

Tyne nodded. "Yes, I should have. I mean, that was one of the main reasons I finally got out of the Company. It got to be too much, seeing people you've grown close to taken out, usually in the worst possible ways."

"Yeah," Lyons whispered hoarsely. "That's the way it happens all right."

The two of them fell silent for a moment, each lost in their private thoughts and memories.

IN THE COCKPIT, pilot Sam Hurst took the Corsair up higher, keeping his eyes on the instrument panels as he talked with Blancanales.

"No offense, but I think you guys are all crazy as loons for doing this."

"What makes you say that?" Blancanales asked.

"Hey, I know what happened last time down there on that island," Hurst said. "Y'ask me, it was a damn lucky thing those cannibals didn't swoop in and haul away Meisner and the lady back there. They like white meat, you know."

Blancanales rolled his eyes and shook his head. "You been reading too many comic books, Sammy. The Doteine aren't cannibals. They aren't even head-hunters."

"What makes you so sure, huh?"

Before Blancanales could answer, the jet was buf-feted by turbulence and Hurst turned his full concen-tration to the controls, jockeying to stabilize the craft. Just as quickly as it started up, however, the air calmed and the plane leveled off. Hurst whistled low, then carried on as if nothing had happened. "I mean, the way I see it, there haven't really been any extensive studies of the interior tribes, so who's to say they aren't cannibals and headhunters? Think about it."

"I'll try not to, actually," Blancanales said as he turned back to the map. "We'll have enough real ob-stacles to deal with without inventing any."

"Suit yourself," Hurst said. "It's your funeral."

"Not if we can help it."

"Then there's that tropical storm blowing in," the pilot said. "Supposed to be a real humdinger. Noth-ing you want to be out wandering in."

"I think we packed a few umbrellas," Pol said.

"Go ahead, make fun," Hurst said. "But I'm tel-lin' ya, these babies are rough stuff. Look, I can even see it starting to roll in."

Peering through the windshield, Blancanales saw a dark band of clouds crowding above the horizon. "We checked that storm out, and it's supposed to sweep a few hundred miles south of the island. Won't be our problem."

Hurst smiled knowingly. "You obviously haven't spent much time in the Caribbean. Storm rolls into this neck of the woods, it's got a mind of it's own. They take some kinda perverse pleasure in making the weatherman look bad."

"We'll keep that in mind," Pol promised.

The jet's radio crackled to life and Blancanales recognized the voice of Aaron Kurtzman. "Stony Man to A-T One. Do you read?"

"Naw," Blancanales quipped as he keyed the microphone. "I usually wait for the movie to come out."

"Ah, Pol. In fine humor as always."

"What's up, Bear? Besides us."

"Well, that's part of what I was calling about," Kurtzman told him. "You guys just missed a chance to link up with Kissinger and Grimaldi."

"What? I thought Cowboy was out of commission."

"He should be, but he's got it in his head that there's some kind of conspiracy or something behind Meisner's death and he wanted to look into it personally."

"Well, we aren't about to swing back to pick 'em up," Blancanales said. "We're more than halfway to the island."

"That's fine. Cowboy wanted to concentrate on Miami first anyway. If he can shake off the flu he and Jack might head down to Skyler's later on."

"That would come in handy," Pol said, "especially if they can bring a plane with 'em. This Coast Guard tub is due back after we're dropped off, so we'll need a lift in a couple of days."

"I'll pass the word along. Should be no problem, though. I'll have them aim for the day after tomorrow."

"Good. With any luck, by then we should be back from our little field trip with a roll of shots of these koupreys."

"Take care down there, Pol," Kurtzman advised.

"Don't worry," Pol said, grinning at the pilot, "I'm too tough to chew and I was never one to go to a shrink."

"Huh? What are you talking about?"

"Never mind, Bear," Blancanales said. "Look, if you talk to Cowboy or Grimaldi later, tell 'em they can try to reach us by radio but the reception out at Skyler's Island is supposed to be pretty wretched, and word is there's going to be another storm rolling in to make things worse."

"We know that," Bear said. "That's why we wanted to get through to you before you were too far over the Caribbean."

"You have some other news or something?"

"Well, Phoenix Force caught wind of a rumor out of Beirut that Moscow has more than a passing interest in Skyler's Island. Nothing specific, but there was apparently some kind of money transfer run through a KGB shadow company there and Hokes's name came up, along with mention of some kind of stepping stone to Central America."

"Hmm," Blancanales mused. "Sounds a little too close for comfort. We'll definitely check it out."

Kurtzman passed along a few more messages from the Farm, then signed off. As he set back the microphone, Pol glanced over at Hurst. "I don't know about cannibals, but it sounds like maybe there *is* something going on down there that we don't know about."

13

"Nice sunset, eh?"

Kissinger looked off to his right and nodded. As it slipped beneath the Gulf of Mexico, the sun left behind long horizontal clouds that took on shades of purple, brown and burnt orange. "Yeah," he said, reaching for a handkerchief and blowing his congested nose. "Really chokes me up."

"Hey, you're the one who wanted to crawl out of the sick bed, so spare me the complaints," Grimaldi taunted as he sped above the coral reefs of Florida Bay, bound for the Keys. "And if we don't get a bite to eat soon, *I'm* the one who's gonna turn ornery."

"We're almost there," Kissinger said, gazing at a Florida map in the twilight. "And I already said I'd buy dinner, so humor me, okay?"

"You picking up the bar tab, too?"

"If you insist."

"I do."

"Fine. Just space 'em out so you can still drive, okay?" Kissinger set the map down on the dashboard and fought back a yawn. The yawn won. For all the sleep he'd had back at the hotel in Virginia, he found it hard to believe that now he could be so bone weary with exhaustion.

"Hell, after some food and drink, I'll be in fine shape to ride this sucker all the way to Key West." Grimaldi patted the dashboard. "Whaddya say, Cowboy? We can whoop it up and mail Schwarz a postcard to let him know what he passed up to go tromping through the jungle."

"No thanks," Kissinger said. "Closest I see myself to whooping it up is coming down with whooping cough."

The two men continued railing one another for another five miles, after which Grimaldi exited onto Fiddler Key and followed side roads to the coast. They stopped at a service station and found out that Juan Jaisez's address was on the aged Shivering Timbers pier. As they pulled into the parking lot, a few random stars were winking into life in the night sky overhead and a three-quarters moon broke through the clouds to cast its reflection on the gulf waters that came lapping into shore. Most of the fishermen and tourists had left the pier, but there were a dozen cars and ten low-slung Harleys in the parking lot, and from the sounds of it everyone was gathered near the end of the pier at the bar and grill. A jukebox was blaring a song by Jimmy Buffett, patron saint of the Keys, and drunken voices bawled the chorus out into the bay as Kissinger and Grimaldi walked down the docks to Jaisez's enclosed residence.

Their first knock on the locked front gate brought Cortez to his feet and the rottweiler drowned out the noise from the bar with its protective yelps.

"Nice peaceful place here, huh?" Grimaldi deadpanned as he beat his knuckles on the gate a second time.

Kissinger grimaced slightly and pressed his fingertips against the side of his head, trying to hold a headache in check. "Yeah, right," he groaned. "Something tells me this isn't where Otis Redding wrote 'Dock of the Bay.'"

Standing on his tiptoes, Grimaldi peered over the top of the gate. Behind the slavering rottweiler, the small shack was dark. "Well, Cowboy, looks like we're batting a thousand today. Nobody home."

"Shit," Kissinger muttered, giving the fence a light kick and earning another round of yelps from the guard dog.

"Tell you what," Grimaldi suggested. "How about we grab a bite next door and check back on the way out?"

Kissinger looked in the direction of the dive. A drunk stumbled out of the bar and clung to a handrail as he stepped down to the docks. "I don't know, Jack," Cowboy murmured. "I kinda had my heart set on something a little more . . . sedate."

Grimaldi gave his cohort a good-natured jab. "C'mon, Cowboy. Toughen up already. You gotta meet this flu on its own terms. Grab the bull by the horns."

"Nut up and do it," Kissinger said.

"Damn straight," Grimaldi asserted, ignoring his friend's sarcasm. "Let's go. Live a little."

"Die is a little more like it," Kissinger muttered.

"That's the spirit."

Inside, the Shivering Timbers Bar and Grill was every bit as run-down and rowdy as expected. The walls and ceiling were covered with old fishing gear and boat tackle tangled up in drooping lengths of fishnet. There were only seven tables, all of them taken, and a small crowd was crammed into the corner by the jukebox, watching a game of pool being played on a warped table. Masking tape covered tears in the felt. The atmosphere was that of a watering hole frequented by a loyal band of locals, and both Kissinger and Grimaldi felt themselves being scrutinized as they inched through the throng and made their way to two vacant stools at the bar.

"Cheery ambience, I'll say that much," Grimaldi drawled over the din. "Folks here seem real fond of strangers."

The bartender came over to them, wiping an empty beer pitcher with an off-white towel. He was tall, thick around the middle, with tattooed hula girls straddling anchors on his hairy biceps. "What'll it be?" he asked.

"Pair of cold ones for starters." Grimaldi pointed to the draft spigots behind the big man. "And what kind of fast food do you have?"

"Got some seafood gumbo," the bartender said. "House speciality."

"Spicy?" Kissinger said.

"You bet. Put hair on your chest and cure whatever ails you."

"Good, I'll have a bowl."

"Make that two," Kissinger said. As an afterthought, he added, "Say, you wouldn't happen to know anything about the guy who lives in that shack next door, would you?"

The bartender set down the pitcher and eyed both men suspiciously as he started filling a pair of frosted beer steins. "Who wants to know?"

"Old friends," Grimaldi lied. "Juan and I go way back."

"That so?" The tender set out the men's drinks. "Well, I ain't seen him lately. You're such good friends with him, maybe you might want to square away the beer tab he's stuck me with."

"I'm not that close," Grimaldi wisecracked. "Did he by any chance drop by here after he got back from that expedition down on Skyler's Island?"

"I wouldn't know," the tall man said. "It ain't like he comes in here to talk shop, y'know? 'Scuse me, I got some other folks to tend to. Be right back with the soup."

Kissinger and Grimaldi sipped their beers as the bartender took another order down at the end of the bar, then pushed through a swinging door to the kitchen. Just before the door swung shut, Kissinger could see the man reach for a telephone on the kitchen wall.

"Think he's hiding something?" Grimaldi asked.

"I'm not sure," Kissinger confessed. "Might want to keep an eye on him, though."

They turned their attention to the nearby pool table, where a short fat man in a polyester suit was making fast work of a ponytailed biker in a game of eight ball. Although most of the other people watching were obviously friends of the biker, the fat man showed no sign of uneasiness. Pausing only long enough for a puff on his cigarette between shots, he sank five balls in quick succession, finishing with a tidy bank shot of the eight. He beamed at his sullen-faced opponent, then looked to the other bikers and said, "Next."

The biggest of the spectators broke away from the others and put two quarters into the table's coin slots, then gave the mechanism a quick jerk, releasing the balls for another game. As he racked them up, the biker glowered at the fat man, who nonchalantly chalked his cue.

"Guy's got some balls," Grimaldi said.

"Yeah, and not just on the table," Kissinger replied.

The bartender returned with two huge ceramic bowls full of thick, steaming soup. "Need another round to wash 'em down with?" he asked.

Kissinger nodded, then asked, "You know who around here might take messages for Juan? He doesn't have a phone."

The bartender shrugged. "You might wanna check the guy at the first bait shop tomorrow morning."

As the tall man went over to take a drink order from the man in the suit, Grimaldi and Kissinger turned to their gumbo. After one taste, Cowboy grabbed for his beer and took a long swallow. His eyes and nose were running.

"That good, huh?"

Kissinger nodded. "If this doesn't knock that flu on its ass, nothing will."

After getting his drink from the bartender, the fat man returned to the pool table and calmly disposed of his second foe. Kissinger and Grimaldi watched the game between bites, and when they were finished, Cowboy said, "Maybe we better slip out of here before that guy wins one game too many and the fur starts flying."

"Good idea," Grimaldi said.

They paid their bill and headed out of the tavern. Kissinger shook his head in disbelief. "I'll be damned, but that gumbo really did the trick. I feel the best I have in days."

"Great. Up for Key West, then?"

"I don't know about that," Kissinger said. "I think I'd rather quit while I'm ahead and catch some winks at that Motel 6 we saw on the way here."

"Let's try Juan one more time as long as we're here," Grimaldi said, moving over to the gate in front of Jaisez's shack. He knocked again, and Cortez went back into howling mode. The pilot glanced over the fence, then asked Kissinger, "You think maybe we ought to invite ourselves in for a few minutes? We could squeeze around Fido here and have a look at things."

Kissinger glanced around. There was no one else in sight. "Might be a good idea. Maybe we should swing around the back first, though."

"Fine by me."

Circling to the fenced-off area farthest from the tavern, Kissinger and Grimaldi looked around for the easiest point of access. There was a narrow ledge reaching out from the main dock, and the men inched out onto it, holding on to the fence for support. Halfway out, Kissinger tested a section of fence, then said, "I think it'll hold. I'll go up first."

But before Cowboy could pull himself up, a beam of light suddenly flashed their way and someone on the docks called out, "Freeze! Police!"

Kissinger and Grimaldi glanced at one another. Grimaldi shook his head disgustedly. "Me and my great ideas."

"Come this way, slowly," the voice from the docks advised them.

Neither Kissinger nor Grimaldi could see past the harsh glare of the officer's flashlight, and it wasn't until they had inched back to the pier that they realized the uniformed cop was accompanied by a second man—the fat man wearing the polyester suit. He withdrew his wallet and opened it so Kissinger and Grimaldi could see his badge as he introduced himself.

"Sergeant Nipwen, Dade County Sheriff's Department. Up against the wall, gentlemen."

When Kissinger and Grimaldi hesitated, the other officer snapped off his flashlight and held out his service revolver. "Now!" he shouted above the drone of the rottweiler on the other side of the fence.

"Look, fellas..." Grimaldi began to explain.

"I asked you to assume the position," Nipwen interrupted with the same calm he'd demonstrated back at the bar.

"You play a mean game of pool for a cop," Kissinger told him as he turned and spread-eagled against the fence.

"Spare me the flattery," Nipwen said. As the other cop frisked Kissinger, the fat man patted down Grimaldi, coming up with his Government Model .45. "Well, well, what do we have here?"

"What you have here are two special government agents on assignment," Grimaldi snapped. "What you're gonna have is egg on your face if you and your boyfriend don't lighten up."

"ID's in my wallet," Kissinger explained after his gun had been lifted.

"Stay put a second," Nipwen told his prisoners. He instructed the other cop to shine his flashlight on the photostats proclaiming Kissinger and Grimaldi to be official members of a Federal Crime Task Force, one of various covers they used while plying their trade on behalf of Stony Man Farm.

"There's a number there you can call for confirmation," Kissinger called out over his shoulder.

"That's all right," Nipwen said. "At ease, and I guess we owe you an apology."

"Innocent mistake," Grimaldi said as he turned away from the fence and took back his gun and ID.

"It's just that you were asking questions about Juan Jaisez," Nipwen explained. "The bartender called us because our people had asked him to do so earlier. He didn't know I was working undercover at the bar until I collared him after the call."

"And why are you so concerned about Juan Jaisez?" Kissinger asked.

"We wanted to ask him a few questions. Seems two of his friends turned up dead a couple of hours ago," Nipwen explained.

THE BODIES of Dennis Burks and Roger Cravens had been removed from the back room of the Flagler Key marina long before Kissinger and Grimaldi showed up with Sergeant Nipwen to view the scene of the crime. The homicide detectives and coroner had already been by to take care of their business. Chalk outlines marked the spots on the floor where the men had died and there were dried pools of blood within the whitened shapes. The room, used for storage and filled with crates and supplies, was dimly lit by a dangling seventy-five-watt light bulb. One crate, apparently used as a makeshift poker table, had been tipped on its side near one of the victims, and the floor was littered with cigarette butts, spare change, a few dollar bills and poker chips.

"It was murder, no question," Nipwen said. "They each had a handgun on them, freshly fired. Burks took three bullets, Cravens two."

"Poker argument?" Kissinger guessed.

"That's what it looks like," Nipwen said. "Or at least what it's supposed to look like."

"What's that supposed to mean?" Grimaldi asked.

"C'mere," Nipwen said, heading over to the stacks of crates along the north wall. He crouched, balancing his weight precariously as he ran a finger along the floor at the base of the crates. Standing up, he held the finger under the light so Kissinger and Grimaldi could see the fine traces of white powder mixed in with dirt and sawdust.

"Coke?" Grimaldi guessed.

Nipwen nodded. "And when we brought in our sniff dogs they went crazy just catching a whiff of this residue shit. We figure there was one shitload of stuff here recently. Real recently."

"Then you think this was really a heist that somebody tried to cover up?" Kissinger speculated.

"Yep."

The fat cop brushed his hand off on his pants and led his new colleagues outside. The marina was two islands and two miles away from Fiddler Key, but the other island could be seen in the distance, linked by the dark span of the Overseas Highway. In the nearby waters were dozens of sailboats and cabin cruisers, swaying at their moorings under the yellow glow of halogen security lamps.

"We've had our eye on these guys for a couple of months now," Nipwen explained. "At first they were selling small quantities—nickel-dime shit, but then they started going bigger. We wanted to find out who their supplier was, but they did a good job of covering their tracks and we never came up with a solid lead. The only real connection we made was with this Jaisez guy, but there was no real solid drug angle there—just the fact that he spent a lot of time overseas.

"Our feeling was that if Jaisez was linked to the coke, he might have had something to do with these killings or else the killers might go for him next, for whatever reason."

"And that's who you thought we were," Kissinger guessed.

"Bingo," Nipwen said. They proceeded from the marina to the parking lot, where the sheriff put in a quick call to the officer he'd left behind at Fiddler Key. No one else had shown up at Jaisez's place yet.

On a hunch, Grimaldi asked, "Supposing Jaisez isn't directly linked with any of this but that he's just skipped town. Would you have any way of finding out if he took a plane or anything like that?"

"We're looking into it," Nipwen conceded. "Give me a minute and I'll get an update."

As the sergeant used his radio phone to touch base with his dispatcher, Kissinger and Grimaldi both looked out at the moored ships. "I have a bad feeling about this somehow," Cowboy said.

"Me, too," Grimaldi agreed. "Just a few too many coincidences."

"You mean with this coke stuff and Meisner's sister being with the DEA?"

"Something like that," Kissinger answered. "I'm not sure exactly what it is."

Nipwen hung up his mike and rejoined the men. "Well, no sense holding our breath on Jaisez showing up. He and a buddy of his flew out of Miami early this morning.''

''Where to?'' Kissinger said.

''Can't get our hands on a manifest, so we don't know for sure. One of the airport people thinks he remembers somebody mentioning the Caribbean.''

''Skyler's Island,'' Grimaldi muttered.

''What's that?'' the sergeant asked.

''Never mind,'' the pilot said. ''Excuse me a minute. I've got an important call to make....''

14

Sam Hurst proved to be a better forecaster than the weatherman. Two days ahead of schedule, tropical storm Joe had picked up steam and fury en route to Skyler's Island and was now coming in from the south under cover of night, with the might of an invading army. It had been Hurst's original intent to bring the Coast Guard Corsair down on the airstrip owned by Coastal Sands Inc., but with lightning already streaking down on that side of the island and high winds blowing in at a dangerous angle, he decided it would be safer to make a landing along the north shore. The old weed-choked runway was now property of the country's militia, and within moments after rolling to a stop, the Corsair was surrounded by four jeeps, each containing five soldiers from the nearby barracks. Their headlights were set on bright, illuminating the jet from all sides. The soldiers were brandishing old M-1 carbines.

"I don't see the red carpet," Hurst said as he stared out the windshield.

"I guess they didn't pick up your radio signal announcing our landing, after all," Pol said. "They must think we're an invading force."

Sandy glanced over at Tyne. "Do you think they'd recognize you?"

"I'm not sure, but it's worth a try." Tyne got up from her seat and unlocked the cabin door. Before she could open it, however, Blancanales waved for her to wait.

"Maybe we should just try to talk to them first," he suggested, pulling down a bullhorn from a rack behind the cockpit. "Do they speak English?"

"Some of them do," Tyne said. "I know a little of their language, too, so hopefully I can get us somewhere."

Blancanales handed her the bullhorn and told the others, "It might be a good idea if we all kept a low profile for the time being." He ducked below the nearest window and the others followed suit. As a precaution, the men from Able Team drew their .45s.

Tyne opened the cabin door a crack and pressed the bullhorn against the opening. She called out a few words in Robidi, a language derived from a blend of French and Portuguese and named after the island's capital. There was a pause, during which a distant flash of lightning and the rumble of thunder announced the approaching storm.

"What'd you tell them?" Lyons said.

"I said who I was and told them we landed here because of the weather. And I asked if anyone spoke English."

She was finally answered by a soldier with a deep, booming voice that required no amplification. "Why are you here?"

Tyne called back, "I just told you, because of the weather."

"Why are you coming to the island?"

"I live here," she explained patiently. "I'm with the Coastal Sands consortium. Ask General Timeli. He knows me."

There was another pause. Raindrops began to patter on the roof of the jet. Schwarz braved a peek through one of the windows. "Looks like they're on a walkie-talkie. Let's hope they don't catch the general in a bad mood."

"I just hope they catch him, period," Sandy said. "This sure isn't what I'd call a good omen for the expedition."

"All right," the soldier outside finally hollered after a rattle of thunder. "You come out, one at a time, hands on your heads."

Blancanales looked at the others as he holstered his automatic. "Well, should we go unarmed, too?"

"Much as I hate to, I think so," Lyons said. "Those M-1s are prehistoric, but they've got enough of them to do us all in a few times over if they want to. I don't think we have any choice but to put our trust in Tyne's clout with the general."

Schwarz unfastened his holster and tossed it in the chair he'd been sitting in. "I'll go first," he said, throwing open the door. "We aren't going to be able to climb all the way down with our hands over our heads, but hopefully they won't be too picky."

Lyons followed him down onto the wing, then to the ground. The wind was beginning to pick up and the rain came down at a slant, stinging their faces as they helped Hurst and their fellow passengers down. Two of the jeeps circled around from the other side of the plane and five of the soldiers marched forward to keep a closer eye on the new arrivals. Their spokesman was a compact, muscular man in combat fatigues.

"I apologize for the inconvenience," he told them, "but this is most irregular."

Hurst glanced up at the dark night sky, where two shafts of lightning zigzagged down over the jungle interior a few miles away. "And that storm's most nasty," he told the officer. "How about if we get somewhere dry before we all get our butts zapped."

The officer motioned to the barracks, a plain one-story structure at the edge of the airfield. "The general will see you there."

The expedition party fell into single file, flanked by the jeeps. As they started for the barracks, Sandy whispered, "My brother mentioned this general. He's probably going to want some money."

Hurst hummed a few bars of "The Wedding March" and sang under his breath, "Here come the bribes ... and I hope he takes credit cards."

The lead soldier shone a flashlight in Hurst's eyes and warned him, "You could be shot for that, you realize."

"Obviously not," Hurst replied before falling silent.

As they continued, Tyne spoke to the others. "I know the general. Let me deal with him one-on-one and I'm sure we can clear all this up."

GENERAL TIMELI leaned closer to his bathroom mirror and trimmed the hairs of his mustache, then stood back to eye the results of his handiwork. Not bad, he had to admit. For a man of forty-five, he still fancied himself quite the physical specimen, a man capable of rousing lust in a woman and sating that lust with passionate abandon. He had long lost track of his bedroom conquests during his six years as the muscle behind Prime Minister Mayos. Dozens? Easily.

"You stud," he told his reflection.

He smiled and let out a deep, sonorous laugh. Holding his breath, he made a fist and pounded it repeatedly against the hardened muscles of his bare stomach. Barely a tickle for a man as strong as he.

The storm was now raging over the militia compound, rain pelting the roof. Timeli slipped into a silk smoking jacket and flinched slightly as a peal of thunder rattled the windows beside him. He imitated the boom with a roar of his own, then broke out laughing again as he crossed the room to the wet bar and poured himself a tall bourbon. His quarters, only a short march from the austere surroundings of the barracks, were decidedly more lavish, from the thick-piled rugs to the paneled walls and the collection of antique vases resting on various stands throughout the main room. And this was only the tip of the iceberg compared to the splendor of his hacienda in the mountains fourteen miles away. Oh, if his men knew about that . . .

There was a sharp, staccato rapping on the door.

Timeli drained his bourbon, then called out, "What?"

"The woman is here," came the voice on the other side of the door.

"Ahh." Timeli gave himself a final once-over in the mirror, then tightened the sash on his smoking jacket and announced, "Send her in."

Tyne Murray was wet from the storm, her hair curling tightly around her head. She closed the door behind her and took a few steps into the room, keeping her distance from the general.

"Ms Murray," Timeli said, sauntering to the bar. "You are a Scotch drinker, yes?"

"Normally, yes," she responded coolly. "What I'd like now, however, is an explanation."

"Explanation?"

"You know what I'm talking about, dammit!"

"The reception you received? Is that what's troubling you?"

"Don't patronize me, General."

"But, of course. You would have had us greet you and these strangers as if you were all royalty, yes? Is that it? We should all jump for joy that you've brought more people to sniff around where they don't belong."

Tyne took a step to one side, running her finger around the rim of a vase. "It couldn't be helped. They were coming regardless of what I said. I had to come with them." She looked up at the general. "And we're just going to have to make the best of it."

"Oh? And what do you suggest? Perhaps we should take a cue from your friends in the consortium and stage another ambush."

"Stage?" Tyne gasped. "What are you talking about?"

"Who is being patronizing now, Ms Murray, hmm?" Timeli laughed again, eyes twinkling with amusement. "You white people think you are so shrewd and we islanders are so ignorant. It really amazes me."

Tyne was taken aback, and although she tried not to betray it, Timeli could see her uneasiness.

"Do you really think we aren't aware that Stephen Hokes has Colombians on his property?" he asked her casually. "That he wants more land so that he can plant cocaine?"

Tyne quietly drew in a deep breath and circled around Timeli to the bar. It took all her concentration to keep her hands steady as she poured herself a glass of Scotch from a crystal decanter. Suddenly everything had changed. She had come in expecting to curry favor with the general with a small bribe. But now...now it was clear that the stakes had been raised significantly. It was time to reevaluate allegiances, to see where she stood.

A flash of lightning touched down near the airfield and thunder reverberated through the room. The inside lights flickered several times but remained on. Timeli opened a humidor and withdrew a gold-leafed cigarette. As he fit it into an ivory holder, he looked at Tyne, calmly awaiting her response.

"How long have you known?" she finally managed to ask.

Timeli shrugged as he lit his cigarette. "Oh, almost from the beginning. But you know how it is with a partnership...you learn to overlook certain matters in the name of a greater good."

"So all this while you've just been playing along?"

"Me? Yes." Timeli blew a plume of smoke. "The prime minister, however, is another matter. He doesn't yet have a complete grasp of the big picture. And I certainly don't wish to confuse him with the facts, as you Americans are so fond of saying."

"But why haven't you come forward?"

"No reason to." Timeli gestured around the room. "We have our power and adequate comforts. The Cartel is useful to us, so we let them think they are being clever. They have the connections and expertise to set up the kind of operation we could only have dreamed of. Once things have been established and the profits are coming in, then perhaps we will have to have a little heart-to-heart with Mr. Hokes. But not now.''

''Why are you telling me all this?'' Tyne asked.

''First, because I like you,'' Timeli confessed. ''You are very mature and *very* attractive. I like that in a woman. Second, we would like to have someone who understands our position well placed within the Cartel. Just to keep things in check.''

''You want me to spy on them?''

''It is your calling, after all....''

Tyne helped herself to one of the cigarettes from the humidor. The general lit it for her.

''And if I don't want to go along with you?''

''That is your choice, of course,'' Timeli sighed. ''But I think you will, if only to make sure that we help keep secret your little part in the untimely demise of some of Juan Jaisez's friends back in Florida.''

Tyne was shocked anew. ''What?'' she sputtered.

''Apparently Mr. Hokes called you to say Jaisez was back on the island trying to play out of his league. He was threatening to reveal certain information about the Cartel, information that was in the hands of some trusted friends by the names of—''

''I know their names,'' Tyne snapped angrily.

''Yes, you do. And so will the police eventually. Fortunately you handled the job very well. Hardly any incriminating evidence was left behind, aside from a few loose traces of cocaine.''

Tyne had no idea how the general had managed to discover her role in the executions of Juan Jaisez's marina cohorts. But she knew that she would never underestimate the man again...not if she ever planned to leave the island alive.

"We need to discuss what to do with this new expedition," she told the general. "I think we should arrange for another ambush, only this time we need to be less tentative. There have to be more deaths."

"No, I don't think so," Timeli said. "The Cartel wouldn't want it, and we certainly don't want to alienate them."

"Then what? I can't just lead them all around the island and hope they don't stumble onto something."

Timeli stubbed out his cigarette and loosened the sash of his smoking jacket as he strode toward the woman. "We can think of something later. For now, let us officially acknowledge our partnership... yes?"

WHILE TYNE WAS WITH the general, the others were held in an old unlit service bay near the barracks. Rain seeped through innumerable holes in the roof and dropped noisily into growing puddles along the oil-stained floor. The prisoners were forced to either stand or sit on sagging cardboard boxes filled with tiles that had been purchased to fix the roof six years ago.

"Maybe we should patch them together into umbrellas so we can keep dry," Lyons said cynically as he kicked the tiles and went back to pacing the damp enclosure. He ventured near one of the windows and glanced out, watching a pair of guards posted under a large overhang, M-1s cradled in their arms. Beyond them the barracks stood out like a black hulk, with only a few lights shining within. General Timeli's quarters were not visible from the bay. "What's taking her so long, dammit?"

"You know how tin-star big shots are in backwaters like this," Hurst said. "He's probably got her waiting outside while he watches some *Green Acres* rerun he picked up on his satellite dish." The pilot went through his pockets for a match and struck one, holding his watch close to the flame. "She hasn't been gone that long, actually."

"Storm's letting up," Gadgets said, hearing the distant drone of thunder. "Any luck and we'll have decent weather when we go trekking, provided we get things squared away with the *federales* here."

"All that rain's going to make for a real mess in the jungle," Blancanales grumbled. "Remember what Tyne was saying about flash floods wiping out trails?"

"We'll manage somehow," Sandy said.

"The floods could actually work in our favor," Schwarz speculated.

Sandy looked at Gadgets hopefully. "You think so?"

Schwarz nodded. "Pol's probably right about the trails being wiped out, but by the same token, the wider the river, the farther we'll be able to take it into the jungle. We might even end up making better time."

"I hope you're right," Lyons said, "but it sounds like wishful thinking to me."

They talked back and forth a few minutes longer, during which time the rain ceased and leaks stopped dripping down from the old ceiling. Then they heard the sound of approaching footsteps. Hurst went to the window and looked out. "It's her."

The huge rolling door to the service bay was opened from outside and Tyne appeared in silhouette against the twin beams of two flashlights.

"We're all set," she told them. "There's a small hotel just past the outpost. We can stay there. The general's picking up the tab."

"How'd you manage that?" Schwarz said as he and the others headed out into the open.

"I just took him to task for giving us this prisoner-of-war treatment," Tyne explained. "He doesn't want to run afoul of the consortium, so when I mentioned they'd be upset when they learned the kind of greeting we'd been given, he asked to make amends."

"Thank heaven for small favors," Blancanales said. He started in the direction of the plane. "Let's get our things."

"Fine," Tyne said. "But just toiletries and a change of clothes, okay? This place we're staying at isn't exactly the Hilton, so it'd be best if we traveled light. They'll keep an eye on the plane."

"That's what I'm afraid of," Blancanales said. "I don't want to come back in the morning and find out they've helped themselves to a little 'bonus' for all their troubles."

Hurst pitched in, "And I want to make sure there's a plane here for me to fly back tomorrow."

"It'll be okay," Tyne insisted. "I promise."

When they reached the Corsair, Lyons stayed behind with Tyne while the others boarded to get their necessities. "So it went okay? Really?" he asked her.

Tyne nodded. "Yeah, fine."

"You seem a little distant."

"I can't help it," Tyne said. "I was bluffing my way through a lot of it. I had this fear Timeli was going to call me on it, and who knows what would have happened..."

"Bluffing? How so?"

"I said the consortium was backing this expedition, too, when that's not really the case," Tyne told him.

"I know," Lyons said. "They're afraid of the publicity another attack by the natives could bring."

"Right. Well, I managed to convince the general that wasn't the case. So, for now, we're doing all right. We're just going to have to make some changes in our plans, that's all."

"What kind of changes?"

Tyne saw Sandy climbing down from the jet with her bags. She gestured for the other woman to hand her things down, then told Lyons, "We can discuss it later, okay?"

15

Kissinger dreamed he was on an expedition with Clark Meisner. They were drenched in sweat and covered with scratches from having to make their way bare-handed and barefoot through an impregnable sea of razor-edged savanna. It seemed as if they had been marching for hours and still there was no sign of relief. A faint wind was blowing, making the grass bend and undulate around them in all directions, like waves on a pale green sea. To keep their spirits up, they were singing popular songs and substituting bawdy lyrics. Suddenly a gigantic ebony figure rose into view directly in front of them, holding a long shaft of bamboo the size of a baseball bat. The apparition raised the shaft to his lips and blew. Kissinger lunged to his right, pushing Meisner aside as a dart whistled past and ripped through the surrounding grass where they'd been standing seconds before. Stumbling to their feet, the men began to flee, but a second giant loomed into view, blocking their way and launching another projectile at them. Kissinger ducked clear but Meisner took the dart in the chest, groaning as it thudded into him, piercing flesh and tissue en route to his heart. As Kissinger hurriedly pulled the dart from his friend's chest, the two men looked at each other.

Meisner had a stunned, fearful look on his face. Then his expression went blank and he slumped into the grass. Kissinger looked around apprehensively and saw that there were now four giants closing in on him, and no matter which way he turned he saw blowguns aimed at him and the cheeks of the giants filling with air as they prepared to let fly with the darts....

The phone jangled to life on the nightstand by Kissinger's bed. With a jolt, he sat upright and clawed for the receiver. The nightmare was already fading from memory, although Cowboy could feel a tense, over-powering sense of foreboding.

"Hello?"

"Cowboy?" It was Aaron Kurtzman. "I wake you up?"

"That's okay," Kissinger said, glancing at his watch on the nightstand. Seven-thirty. Sunlight was starting to pour through the shades of the hotel room, falling on the figure of Grimaldi dozing in the other bed. They were back in Miami, having left the Keys shortly before midnight without having been able to reach Able Team on Skyler's Island.

"I've tried raising them a half-dozen times," Bear explained, "but they had one doozy of a storm down there and there's just no way to get through."

"Damn!" Kissinger said. "We don't want to head down there until we cover a few more bases here."

"How's the flu?"

For the first time since he'd awakened, Kissinger realized that the mild fever and aching that had plagued him all week was gone. His head was a little congested, but it was nothing compared to what he'd suffered through earlier. "I guess I've found a cure," he told Kurtzman. "Seafood gumbo."

"As long as you don't have to have it for breakfast."

"I don't think so, Bear. Anything else?"

"Well, I did call around and find out how to get in touch with the coroner who did Meisner's autopsy. He should be at work by eight-thirty and he'll be expecting you."

"Great. Hopefully he can give us something we can use."

"What about those murders down at the marina? Any link?" Kurtzman asked.

"There's some kind of connection all right," Kissinger said. "To Jaisez, too, from the look of it. And we found out he doubled back to Skyler's Island before the Team did. We're not sure why yet, but we don't like the way it's shaping up."

"Well, if there's anything more we can do up here at the Farm, let us know, okay?"

"Have 'em put in some overtime on that gym," Kissinger suggested. "Especially the saunas. My sinuses are going to need some pampering once this is all over."

"I'll see what I can do." Kurtzman chuckled.

Kissinger hung up and glanced over at Grimaldi, who was just getting out of bed and stretching. "Looks sunny outside. Nice day to visit the morgue...."

RAFAEL BIS WAS a handsome man with short curls of dark brown hair framing his rugged, chiseled features. He wore his beard at a fashionable two-day's growth and had dark, mirthful eyes. He was hardly the sort of man one normally envisioned as a county coroner. And yet there he was, wearing a white laboratory jacket and laminated name tag as he led Kissinger and Grimaldi down the hallway to his office. He even winked at one of the young women serving as assistants in the pathology wing of the morgue.

"Sorry I missed you yesterday," Bis apologized with a faint Cuban accent. "But if you had seen the lady who offered to take me deep-sea fishing, you'd be wondering why I'm back so early."

"We appreciate your seeing us," Kissinger said as he passed the coroner and stepped into Bis's office, a nondescript room whose walls were filled with anatomical charts and framed scrolls attesting to the extensive medical training that had preceded the Cuban's current occupation.

"Well, in my line of work, it's always nice to run into a good mystery," Bis confessed. He gestured for Kissinger and Grimaldi to sit down as he opened a pack of gum and began unwrapping individual sticks.

"Then there was something mysterious about Meisner's death?"

"Yes and no." Once Bis had five sticks rolled together, he popped the wad into his mouth and began chewing. "Just gave up smoking last week," he explained. "Dissected one too many ravaged lungs, I guess."

"About the yes and no..." Kissinger prompted.

"Yeah, right." Bis went over to a bank of file cabinets, using a key to unlock one. He began searching through drawers as he talked. "Well, we figured out what kind of poison did him in. Too late to help him unfortunately, but such is life, right?"

"And death," Grimaldi said testily. He found the coroner's disaffected airs aggravating and it was all he could do to hold himself in check. "We're in a bit of a hurry, Doctor, so is there any chance we could speed this up?''

"No problem." Bis found the file he was looking for and blew a bubble as he circled around his desk and slumped into the leather embrace of his swivel chair. He skimmed the documents inside the file, then glanced up at the other two men. "The poison's from a plant called Bard's Tongue. Extremely potent little bastard. Here's what it looks like."

He handed Kissinger a photo of a small green-leafed plant whose flower looked amazingly like a long pink tongue with small nodular growths running along the inner folds.

"Looks like something out of *Little Shop of Horrors*," Grimaldi said as he eyed the photo over Kissinger's shoulder.

"It does, doesn't it?" Bis said, blowing a bubble the same color as the Bard's Tongue. "Won't eat you, but you get its poison inside you and you'll be just as dead as if it had."

"And is there an antidote?" Kissinger wondered.

"To a small extent," Bis said. "If it can be properly diagnosed during the first nine hours after it's entered the system, there's a counter serum that can reduce most of the damage."

"But they didn't diagnose Clark Meisner in time, obviously," Grimaldi said.

Bis shook his head. "Even if we had had reason to suspect this particular poison, it was nearly twelve hours by the time he was brought into the hospital. They'd called ahead to Poison Control in Atlanta with symptoms, but the connection wasn't made."

"Why not?" Kissinger wanted to know.

Bis took the photo of the plant back and returned it to the file. "Well, up to now, the only known habitat for Bard's Tongue was New Guinea, and even there it doesn't exactly grow like a weed, you know? Considering that Guinea's a good few thousand miles away from Skyler's Island, nobody had reason to suspect it was involved."

"Obviously they were mistaken," Grimaldi said. "Like this whole thing with the koupreys."

"Not necessarily," Bis said.

"What do you mean?" Kissinger snapped. "You just said that—"

"Hear me out, okay?" Bis held up one hand like a traffic cop signaling a stop. "Let's remember that Meisner didn't bend over and sniff one of these plants or chop it up and put it on his cereal for breakfast. He got hit by a dart and the dart was obviously dipped in the poison."

"Right," Grimaldi said, "and it's just as obvious that the natives needed to have access to a plant in order to get the poison. Remember, they aren't really the cosmopolitan type, so it's not likely they picked up a little Bard's Tongue from some New Guinea apothecary while they were on vacation, know what I mean?"

Bis grinned and popped another bubble. "Good point. But supposing someone brought the poison to them? Or that maybe someone besides a native fired that dart, wanting Meisner to die a slow death for some strange reason."

Kissinger and Grimaldi looked at each other. The coroner might have been a little on the eccentric side, but he clearly had a keen mind on his shoulders and they had to concede the validity of his argument. They went over the rest of the autopsy report without unearthing any other information of much value, then thanked Bis for his help and left his office.

"Well," Grimaldi speculated as they headed down the main corridor, "I suppose if we could find out the names of everyone who's taken out traveling papers to New Guinea over the past few months, the list couldn't be too long. What do you figure, a couple thousand?"

"At least," Kissinger said, pausing once they reached the phones. "And there's only one way to whittle down a list like that."

Dialing a long-distance number, Kissinger passed the security gauntlet and got through to Stony Man Farm in a little under six minutes. When Kurtzman picked up the other end, Cowboy told him, "I hope you've got those computers warmed up, Bear, 'cause we've got a nice chunk of data for them to chew on."

16

Tyne Murray was right about the Macaw Hotel. Nobody was going to find it ranked very highly in the travel guides, provided it was listed at all. Accommodations were spartan at best, consisting of sunbleached canvas army cots, splinter-filled chairs made of old factory skids and hole-pocked mosquito netting stretched across paneless windows that kept neither mosquitoes nor rain out of the rooms. The odor of mildew permeated the air but was a welcome scent compared to the noxious aroma wafting from the pair of half-rotted wooden outhouses serving as toilet facilities for all boarders at the fourteen-room establishment. Sandy and Tyne had the luxury of a room to themselves, while Able Team and Sam Hurst were forced to share a cubicle with barely enough space for their four cots. Despite the lack of amenities, however, once the storm had passed and they settled in for the night, most of the group had managed to fall quickly asleep.

Blancanales was the first to awaken a scant five hours later, and as he stood up he groaned at the stiffness in his limbs, due no doubt to sleeping on an undersized cot near an opened window. Joints are getting rusty, amigo, he told himself as he did a few leisurely stretches, then left the other men to their sleep and headed down the main corridor of the hotel. The floorboards creaked under his weight and several doors opened as he passed, with tenants peering curiously out at him. He ignored their stares and moved outside, where the sun was just rising above the treetops.

There was an old hand pump near the outhouses, and Blancanales jockeyed it back and forth, grimacing at the high-pitched shriek of unoiled hinges. The first flow of water to sputter out was brackish and foul smelling, and even after he continued pumping, the color and smell improved only a little. Taking care to keep his mouth tightly closed, Blancanales splashed a few drops on his face, then stretched again as he looked down a two-lane dirt road that led to the capitol, a few short blocks away. Robidi was clearly not a city of great wealth. There were only a few buildings that showed any semblance of durability, and there were no automobiles on the unpaved streets, where chickens and stray dogs roamed with idle impudence. Most of the shops were part tent, part shack, offering handmade goods and produce. A few villagers were already out browsing the stalls, matched by an equal number of uniformed militia standing idly about with their carbines slung over their shoulders.

Blancanales was reminded a little of his childhood in the barrios of East L.A. and San Ysidro, and also of poor peasant villages on the Central American mainland, where impoverished families lived in crowded squalor, eking out a feeble existence in the nearby fields and living in constant fear of the state police. No wonder all the resort development was taking place on the other side of the island, away from such reminders that there were those with problems far more serious than the business pressures the wealthy sought a temporary escape from, he thought. Here were people whose only escape from travail came when they were laid six feet under.

"Real fun city, isn't it?" Sam Hurst said as he emerged from the hotel, rubbing a kink in his neck. "I sure hate to leave it all behind, but I'm due back in the States. You want to come clear the rest of your things out of the plane so I can take off?"

"Sure."

As the two men backtracked toward the militia airfield, Hurst said, "You want me to give word to your people that you touched down here instead of the other side?"

"Let me check the radio first," Pol said. "If I can get through, I'd rather talk with them directly. There are a few things we're waiting word on."

At the gateway to the militia base, Hurst and Blancanales showed tags they'd been given the previous night to allow them access to the plane. Out in front of their barracks, two dozen soldiers were doing calisthenics under the watchful eye of their commanding officer. The man who had dealt with the expedition party upon their arrival was nowhere to be seen, however.

"You up for a wager on the expedition?" Hurst asked Blancanales as they walked.

"What kind of wager?"

"I'll bet you it's a bust, and not the drug kind," Hurst said. "No koupreys, no Hokes, no Commies in the brush."

"Okay," Blancanales said. "You're on. How much?"

Before Hurst could reply, they were interrupted by a loud, pained scream coming from the service bay where the expedition party had been briefly held hostage the night before. When the cry was repeated, the two men veered from the plane and went to investigate. Circling the bay, they looked in through the opened door and saw four soldiers looming over four peasants, lashing at them with nightsticks while their superior, the officer Hurst and Blancanales had met the night before, stood off to one side, shouting questions in their native language. The peasants, all teenage boys, cringed on their knees, already bruised and bleeding from their beating. When the truncheons came down again, they let out more anguished howls and pleas for mercy from their tormentors.

"What the hell?" Blancanales exclaimed, drawing the officer's attention. The soldier signaled for his men to ease off their clubs for the moment, then strolled out to meet Blancanales and Hurst.

"Don't stir things up," Hurst warned Blancanales out of the side of his mouth.

Blancanales ignored the advice and stared directly at the officer. "Why are you beating them? They're just kids."

"They are thieves," the officer said calmly. "During the night they scaled one of the fences and broke into your plane."

"What?" Hurst shouted indignantly. "Those bastards!"

"Obviously we caught them before they could get away," the officer said, turning to Blancanales. "But I'm afraid that they dropped some of your equipment as they were fleeing. Your radio was broken, I think beyond repair."

"Damn!" Blancanales swore. Just as quickly, he brought himself under control. "Still, that's not grounds enough for the kind of beating you're giving them. Look at them!"

"You are on Skyler's Island now, not in America," the officer reminded Pol. "We have our own way of dealing with crime and I would have you know that our way has proven more effective than yours. These youths will live, and they will remember what happens to those who break the law. I do not think they will try to steal again. Now, if you will excuse us..."

The officer went back inside the bay, and Hurst dragged Blancanales away as the punishment resumed. "What'd I tell you?" he told Pol. "These people are savages, and that's not even the natives in the jungle. You're in for a rude awakening here, my friend. Mark my words."

FOR BREAKFAST, Lyons and Schwarz nibbled mustard-laden sardines from ration tins they'd packed for the expedition. Between bites, they took sips from their canteens. They were seated on a weathered stone bench outside the hotel, watching a group of small children chase chickens around the parched grounds.

"Looks like fun," Schwarz said.

"Maybe you should ask if you can join in," Lyons suggested.

Gadgets looked at his friend. "Got up on the wrong side of the cot, eh, Ironman?"

Lyons finished one last sardine, then pitched the empty tin into a rusting trash bin and licked mustard from his fingertips. "That obvious, is it?"

"Something's been bothering you since we woke up," Schwarz said. "My guess is that it has to do with a certain female."

"Or maybe it has to do with the mosquitoes I kept swatting all night," Lyons shot back. "Or maybe having to put up with you guys snoring away like the Three Stooges."

Schwarz grinned. "Go ahead, blame it on me if it makes you feel any better. But I know you. You got a jones for Tyne written all over your face. Maybe you should have slept with her back at the plane last night."

Lyons knew that Schwarz had his number. He shrugged and drummed his fingers idly on his canteen. "Don't think it didn't occur to me," he confessed. "But after she came back from seeing the general, she was . . . I don't know . . . standoffish."

"Well, beneath the safari jacket she's a businesswoman, after all," Gadgets theorized. "Having to pull strings with the general and replan this whole expedition on the spur of the moment because of some snag with the prime minister—all that juggling can get someone preoccupied. You also have to consider that she's going back into a jungle where she was ambushed less than a week ago. That can be a little unnerving, I'd imagine."

"Yeah, maybe you're right," Lyons admitted.

"Trust me," Schwarz said. "Once we get this jungle business behind us, you'll be in a better position to see if there's some kind of relationship in it for you."

"And what about you?" Lyons countered. "You and Ms Meisner are something of an item, aren't you?"

"It's mostly on hold, given what's happened to her brother and all. I'm just a friend right now, and that's fine."

"Speaking of Sandy..."

Both men looked toward the hotel. Sandy was on her way out, running a brush through her short blond hair. Spotting them, she waited for the children to run past her, then crossed the yard to the bench.

"Good morning," she told them, offering Schwarz an extra smile. "Where are the others?" she asked, glancing around.

"I think Pol and Hurst went to check on the plane," Lyons answered.

"What about Tyne?"

Lyons looked at Sandy with concern. "She wasn't with you?"

"When I fell asleep she was," Sandy said. "But not when I woke up."

"Maybe she's at the plane, too," Schwarz suggested. "How about we head there ourselves? Hurst said something about wanting to start back for Florida as soon as..."

Gadgets's voice trailed off as he and the others heard an unmistakable droning sound. Glancing in the direction of the militia outpost, they saw the Corsair rise into view from the runway, airborne and Florida bound.

Even as the jet was heading out over the water and vanishing from view, the group was distracted by a second vehicle, this one a jeep bounding slowly along the dirt road linking Robidi with the outpost. Blancanales was riding shotgun and waved to the others as he directed the soldier behind the wheel to stop in front of the hotel. The rest of the supplies for the expedition were stacked high in back.

"Did you manage to get in touch with the Farm?" Lyons asked Pol as they began unloading the jeep.

"Bad news on that front, I'm afraid."

Blancanales went on to explain about the attempted theft and the breaking of the radio, adding, "I asked about using the militia's radio, but they said their transmitter was knocked out by the storm, so no go on that front, too."

"We're really on a good-luck roll, aren't we?" Lyons complained. "I take it Tyne wasn't with you."

Pol shook his head. "Just Hurst. I told him to file a report on our change in plans when he got back to Miami."

The question of Tyne's whereabouts was answered soon after the jeep had been unloaded and was on its way back to the outpost. From the direction of town, a rundown camou-painted truck sputtered into view, with a tall, strangely bearded man at the wheel and Tyne riding beside him in the cabin. Strapped to the sides of the truck were two twenty-foot-long, low-keel rowboats, and in the back rode nine native tribesmen who stared out warily at the village they'd just left and the expedition party they were about to join.

The truck was brought to a stop alongside the stack of supplies. The driver left the engine idling and climbed down to the ground along with Tyne, who introduced him to the group.

"This is Ed Redsana," she told the others. "He was my replacement here on the island when I retired from the Company. A good man."

Redsana nodded a greeting and shook a few hands, then eyed Able Team and said, "Tyne's already briefed me on things, and I've been in contact with your people in the States. In all honesty, I think you're on a wild-goose chase with this whole Stephen Hokes business, and the only Communists we've been able to sniff out are a couple of labor organizers passing out flyers to the construction crews on the other side of the island. But we've pledged to help out, and I think that you might have some luck finding these cows you're looking for, so I took the liberty of filling out your expedition."

"These are Roiyads," Tyne said, gesturing at the men in the back of the truck. "Same tribe as before, but different men. To get them, we had to agree to take a new route to the interior. By our calculations, we should never get closer than within eleven miles of Doteine territory."

"Sounds fine to us," Lyons said on behalf of the Team. "Are we going to drive all the way there?"

Redsana chuckled lightly and shook his head. "I'm afraid that would be somewhat difficult, given all the flooding from the storm. No, actually, I'll be driving you halfway around the island to the mouth of the Aitacon River. You'll transfer to the boats there and head inland. The river might be a little wild because of the rains, but you'll still make better time than you would trying to slog overland."

"Fair enough." Lyons grabbed his knapsack and slung it over the truck railing. "Okay, gang. All aboard," he said.

17

Sergeant Nipwen rode with Kissinger and Grimaldi through the Florida backcountry west of Miami. They had the road to themselves and the calm fields of rolling saw grass stretching out on either side of them struck Kissinger as vaguely familiar. He gradually began to recall the dream he'd had earlier that morning, and an involuntary shudder ran through him as he looked across the flatlands, half expecting giants with blowguns to spring into view at any minute.

"You okay, Cowboy?" Grimaldi asked, noticing his partner's pained expression in the rearview mirror.

"Yeah, fine," Kissinger said.

"Sure about that?"

Kissinger nodded. "Just shaking off the last of that flu."

In the back seat, Nipwen tapped his fingers on his knee. "What I can't shake is this feeling things are finally falling into place."

"I hope you're right," Grimaldi told him. "That why you're wearing your lucky suit?" Grimaldi asked the sheriff's officer as he forced a grin.

Nipwen glanced down at his outfit, a lightweight checkered ensemble that made his garish suit of the night before look almost fashionable. "Hey," he snapped defensively, tugging on his lapels, "I'll have you know this is one of them famous pickle-jar jobs. I could wad it up for a pillow, and come morning there'd still be no wrinkles.''

"Actually, they look more like pajamas than a pillow,'' Grimaldi teased.

Nipwen rolled with the punch. "You're just jealous because I won't give you the name of my tailor.''

Kissinger and Grimaldi had gotten a call from Nipwen after speaking to Kurtzman. Apparently, during the night there'd been some breaks on the double murder in the Keys. Nipwen's people had compared notes with the FBI and DEA and discovered there was a common thread linking the murder victims with recent efforts to shut down the cocaine cartels in Colombia. For details they had been referred to Thad Bonberg, head of the DEA's special agents in Colombia. They were supposed to meet him at eleven at the Everglades training grounds where Able Team had spent the previous day boning up on jungle tactics. It was now 10:59.

"They didn't give you any idea what the connection was?" Kissinger asked Nipwen.

Nipwen shook his head. "You know how territorial these folks can be. Probably thought if he put us on the scent too soon we'd move in and steal some of their headlines.''

"Ah, office politics," Kissinger said. "One of the main reasons I quit the DEA.''

"You were with them?" Nipwen asked. "When?''

"About ten years ago," Cowboy said. "I just couldn't get the hang of playing those games.''

"Cover your ass and brown your nose—and to the top you're bound to goes.''

Kissinger laughed. "Yeah, that was the way it worked."

"Still does," Nipwen said. "Listen, if you guys found a way to get around that, maybe you should pass on the secret, y'know?"

"Not much of a secret," Grimaldi said. "You want to avoid office politics, stay out of the office."

"Yeah," Kissinger added. "We just spend all our time out in the field. When my time's up, I'd rather be stabbed in the back with a knife than a memo."

"Amen to that," Nipwen said.

The entrance to the training grounds wasn't marked, for obvious security reasons, and Grimaldi passed it once before Nipwen caught sight of a telltale landmark that told them they'd gone too far. They backtracked and found the right turnoff, following it back a quarter mile to the main gate, where they were subjected to a detailed search and questioning by the guards, even after they'd presented their credentials and had provided the necessary references to vouch for their legitimacy.

"Sorry for the delay," the head of the detail told them as he finally stepped back and gestured for them to drive through. "It's just that a couple of times over the past three weeks we've had imposters trying to sneak in with false IDs."

"Imposters?" Kissinger questioned.

The guard nodded. "Sent by the big dealers," he explained. "They were hoping to bug the conference and locker rooms, find out how much we know."

"Figures," Grimaldi said, shifting gears into first. "Look, where can we track down Bonberg?"

The guard pointed to a cluster of palm trees inside the grounds. "Over there. He's getting some guys ready for another trip to South Am."

"Thanks."

Grimaldi pulled through the gateway and started down a dirt road leading to the palms. Halfway there, the men heard the familiar rattle of automatic gunfire off in the brush. Suddenly a figure in khaki lunged out into view twenty yards ahead of the rental car. Then, just as suddenly, he was gone, having somersaulted from one side of the road to the other and down a gravel-lined slope leading to a field of mud overlooked by the palm trees. Grimaldi had to slam on his brakes when three other men stormed onto the road, toting M-16s and in apparent pursuit of the first man. One of them waved his rifle at the car for a fleeting second, then shouted for his cohorts to clear the road.

Driving slowly forward, Grimaldi looked off to his right, where Kissinger and Nipwen were already watching the pursued man crawling on his belly beneath row after row of barbed-wire fencing, all the while ducking a steady hail of lead peppering the ground around him.

"Shit, they're using live rounds on that guy!" Nipwen exclaimed, reflexively reaching for his gun.

"Relax," Kissinger said calmly. "Hell, we go through this all the time, and we're still in one piece."

"You should have seen some of the stuff we pulled during that hostage rescue drill we had while you were pulling bed duty," Grimaldi told Kissinger.

"Don't remind me about that," Cowboy said.

At the base of the palms was a small dirt lot filled with dust-laden pickups and jeeps. Grimaldi parked off to one side, leaving the car as shaded as possible.

The men got out and circled around to the end of the barbed-wire obstacle course.

Caked with mud from head to toe, the man in khaki dragged himself up to a spigot poking out from the side of a small concrete bunker. He cranked the handle and splashed water on his face, then fumbled through his pockets for a crumpled pack of cigarettes. Lighting up, he regarded the new arrivals through a cloud of smoke.

"We're looking for Thad Bonberg," Nipwen said.

"That's me normally, but right now my name is mud," Bonberg said. After exchanging introductions with the others, he waved a hand toward the bunker. "C'mon, step into my office."

Inside the concrete enclosure was a plain table and bench seats and a row of lockers. A set of swinging doors led to a small shower stall, and as Bonberg stepped in and began pulling off his clothes, he called out, "Speak up and I'll hear you. I just want to wash off this mud before it ruins my complexion."

"We were told you came up with some kind of connection to those stiffs on the Keys and your cartel buddies," Nipwen said.

"Yep," Bonberg boomed as he stood under the shower and lathered his scalp with shampoo. "The mysterious Stephen Hokes."

"Yeah?"

"Yeah," Bonberg explained, "last night my Bogotá squad staged a mountain raid on a major camp. There was an airstrip up there and they busted things up just as the Colombians were loading up some old DC-3 with coke paste and plant seedlings."

"Coca plants?" Kissinger asked.

"Righto," Bonberg said. "Anyway, we put a little fear of the Lord into the pilot and he gave his tongue a good wag. Said he'd just gotten back from making a similar delivery to...guess where."

"The Keys," Nipwen guessed.

Bonberg made a noise like a game-show buzzer. "Wrong."

"Skyler's Island," Kissinger said.

"Give that man a Kewpie doll!"

"Then what's the connection to our dead boys?" Nipwen asked.

"Just a sec." Bonberg rinsed himself off, then shut off the water and grabbed a towel hanging over the stall doors. "We've made a few arrests while trying to set up the people behind the marina operation. Mostly small dealers. Thing is, every time we get our hands on some crack and coke that hasn't been broken down for the streets, it's always wrapped the same way, in the same kind of paper. Turns out all the stuff in this DC-3 had the same wrapping."

"Aha!" Nipwen exclaimed, snapping his fat fingers. "Then you figure they're trying to shift their operation to the island because of the crackdowns."

"That's about the size of it," Bonberg said as he stepped out of the shower stall, towel wrapped around his waist. He went to one of the lockers and twiddled the combination lock to get at a clean change of clothes. "And we're still waiting on some news from CIA and Interpol to make it official, but our suspicion is that Steve Hokes is the guy the Colombians are working with. Could be the guy's holed up on the island somewhere, pulling all the strings."

"That's the way it adds up for us, too," Kissinger said, going on to relate the background information gleaned by Hal Brognola before he'd put Able Team onto the case.

As he started dressing, Bonberg said, "I'm hopping a plane down to Bogotá this afternoon. Once we've grilled the pilot enough to get some idea of his drop points, I want to put together a force and storm that island with a vengeance."

"I think we're already a step ahead of you on that front," Grimaldi said. "We have some people there, but they've got no idea what they're wandering into."

"Well, if that's the case," Bonberg said, "I hope they have good instincts, because I think the shit's about to hit the fan."

18

Swollen by floodwaters, the Aitacon River flowed wide at its mouth, and the greater width served to weaken the current, helping the expedition to make relatively good time heading upriver toward the interior. Loaded to capacity, each of the long boats sat low in the water, propelled along by the smooth, steady rhythm of the oarsmen, four to each craft. The river was brown from stirred-up sediment and collapsed embankments. Periodically natives positioned at the front of the boats would have to reach out with a pole to prevent collisions with floating pieces of driftwood. Rainwater still pattered down from where it had collected in leaves and branches of the wilting trees that bent over the river.

"I don't know if it's because it's so soon after the storm or just my imagination," Tyne said as she glanced around at the surrounding jungle, "but it seems awfully quiet."

"Probably a little of both," Lyons said. They were sitting toward the back of the second boat, near a pile of supplies. She had her Beretta 424 shotgun balanced across her knees and her Ruger automatic loaded on her hip. Like his Able Team cohorts, Lyons had chosen to rely solely on his Colt .45. They rode along silently a few minutes, lulled by the splash and drag of the oarplay and the gurgle of their wake. Then Lyons turned to the woman. "Is there something else bothering you?" he asked.

"No," she said. "Why, should there be?"

"I don't know," he said. "It just seems that since our dinner date back in Miami things have gone downhill between us."

"I'm sorry," she said, momentarily placing a hand on his knee. "It's just that I guess I'm a little spooked."

"About the expedition or about us?"

"I'm not sure," she said.

Lyons looked away from her a moment, letting his gaze fall on the precision movements of the oar teams in front of him. Farther ahead, he could see Schwarz, Sandy and Blancanales in the lead boat.

"Might be a good idea if we put our social life on the back burner until we're through this," he suggested. "One less ball to juggle."

Tyne smiled faintly. "I think you might be right. Just don't get the idea I'm not attracted to you, because that's not the case."

"The feeling's mutual," he told her. "But I can handle being friends."

"I'm glad," she said. "The last thing I'd want to do is drive you away."

They fell silent again. Tyne absently ran one finger across the checkered stock of her Beretta. She would be glad when this whole charade was over and done with. Keeping up a pretense with Clark Meisner had been strictly a professional arrangement, and his death had bothered her only slightly. But with Lyons it was different. Although she had made advances to him primarily as a ploy to gain what control she could over the return expedition, there was an undeniable attraction, and despite what she'd told General Timeli the night before, she was uncomfortable with the possibility that she might have to play a part in Lyons's death and that of his cohorts.

Hopefully it wouldn't come to that, however. After conferring with Redsana, it had been decided that the best way to resolve the issue would not be to stage another ambush, but rather to make arrangements to bring a handful of kouprey to a grazing area halfway up the river, in the hopes that once Sandy got her photographs the group would be content to call it a successful expedition. Hokes, in the meantime, was making arrangements to fly to Algiers, where he would plant a few misleading rumors and surface long enough to squelch the theory that he was entrenching himself in Skyler's Island. A look-alike was being tracked down by Hokes's people and would be flown to the island, where he'd fortuitously appear in Robidi when the expedition returned from the jungle. The imposter would pass himself off as a technician at one of the rubber plantations, and enough documentation would be fabricated to back up his story and further explain the 'coincidences' that might have led the authorities to think he was Hokes.

If, after all this, Carl Lyons and his group still insisted on sniffing around the island for Communists, arrangements would be made to fly in some expendable group of left-wing terrorists on the promise of giving them sanctuary, then they would be plopped down in a remote section of jungle where the expedition would be directed by a series of planted clues. It was a cumbersome ploy, but all the members of the consortium had agreed it would be the most efficient way to take the heat off the island without jeopardizing their long-range plans. Even the general had agreed to play along with the scenario, a promising sign in Tyne's eyes. If she could place herself strategically between Timeli and Mayos on one side and the Cartel on the other, down the line she could play both sides against the middle and better her own overall position.

By late morning the sky was clear and the sun shone down overhead, reflecting off the river. They'd made their way four miles upriver and had turned onto a tributary far less turbulent than the main artery. On advice from Tyne, the Roiyads' interpreter told the oarsmen to steer to an accessible embankment for a rest break. Able Team eyed the waters for caiman as two tribesmen jumped out of each boat and helped pull them ashore, prows hissing over the soft sand.

"Nice spot," Schwarz said as he climbed out of the lead boat and helped Sandy up to higher ground. She was carrying her brother's Pentax and used it to take several pictures of the beached craft and the expedition party. She'd been shooting all along and had reached the end of the roll.

"Want to help give me some shade?" she asked Schwarz.

"Glad to."

They ventured away from the others, pausing near a thick-trunked tree. Schwarz hunched over, using his body to further block the sun as Sandy cracked open the camera case and removed one roll of film before inserting another. As she worked, she said, "It's funny, but I almost feel like I've been here before. I guess it's just that my brother was always such a good storyteller. The way he'd explain an expedition was so vivid, you'd almost be able to hear and smell these exotic places."

"I'm sure a part of him is with you," Schwarz told her.

"Hopefully the photographer part," Sandy said, closing the camera. "I'd hate it if these shots didn't turn out."

"I'm sure they'll be fine," Schwarz said. "I remember you were taking pictures of ball players for baseball cards when I first met you."

"That was just my cover," she reminded him. "I didn't really have a contract to do that and I was just using one of Clark's old—"

Sandy's sentence was cut short by the sudden sound of gunfire across the river. She and Gadgets exchanged looks of surprise, then rushed back to the embankment, where the others were reacting to a second round of shots.

"What's going on?" Sandy wondered aloud.

"Not sure," Tyne said, dropping to a precautionary crouch and readying her shotgun, "but let's not take any chances."

She told the interpreter to have the tribesmen seek shelter behind the boats while the others fanned out, taking up firing positions along the shoreline. They looked across the river, where the greenery extended all the way to the water's edge. A third volley echoed through the jungle, and two black men in loincloths staggered into view. One collapsed, slumping down the steep embankment, while the other continued running in full flight, splashing into the shallow waters of the river. Spotting the white men, the man waved his arms wildly and shouted in a language they couldn't understand.

"What the hell?" Schwarz muttered, trying to make sense of what he was seeing.

Several of the Roiyad tribesmen peered up at the sound of the man in the river, who waded deeper and deeper, trying to reach the other side. Before he could completely cross, however, there was one last, lone shot and the man's cries were immediately silenced as a bullet smashed into his skull. Going limp in the water, he was carried away from the boats by the gentle current, leaving a red streak in his wake. The other man also slipped into the water and began floating off. His bullet wounds were in the back.

Sounds came from the brush near the river's edge, but whoever had fired the fatal shot stopped short of showing themselves. Blancanales was about to fire a warning shot when Tyne reached out and placed a hand over his gun, telling him, "Don't."

"Why not?" he said. "Those guys were cut down like—"

"It's not our affair," Tyne said.

Lyons overheard the exchange and strode over. "What do you mean, not our affair. Do you know what that was all about?"

Tyne glanced at the bodies, which had already drifted past the bend. She knew they were runaway slaves from Hokes's plantation, but wasn't about to divulge that to the Team. "They're Thiglada, one of the interior tribes," she said. "They were probably either trespassing on another tribe's territory or raiding one of the plantations."

Blancanales wasn't convinced. "There are tribes here with automatic rifles?"

Tyne shrugged. "It wouldn't surprise me. It's not like the twentieth century hasn't come to the island.

But, whatever the case, we'd be making a mistake to get involved. With us on the river and them in the brush, we'd be sitting targets if they decided we were enemy. We have to be realistic here."

Blancanales glanced across the river and grudgingly holstered his Government Model. "You're probably right," he conceded.

Sandy, who had taken photos of the slain natives, lowered her camera and glanced over at the Roiyad tribesmen, who were still huddled behind the boats, fear in their eyes. Their interpreter glanced up at her and said, "Slave hunters. They come for us to be slaves."

"No," Tyne said, stepping in front of Sandy and shaking her head at the interpreter. "That's not true!"

"Slaves?" Schwarz said. "Who around here would have slaves?"

"The plantations, maybe," Lyons guessed.

"That's ridiculous," Tyne said. "Let's not jump to any conclusions, okay? I think it'd be best if we pushed on and got away from here."

Lyons looked at Tyne, troubled by a feeling he couldn't put a finger on. "Is there something more to all this than you're letting on?" he asked.

"Don't start on me," she snapped. "I'm trying to see to it that this expedition comes back in one piece, that's all. Is there anything wrong with that?"

Lyons backed off, putting away his gun. He turned to Blancanales and Schwarz. "She's got a point. Let's get out of here."

19

From the bunker built deep within the Florida Everglades, Thad Bonberg led Nipwen, Kissinger and Grimaldi across the grounds to unit headquarters, a larger and far more sophisticated facility surrounded by towering palmetto trees and discreetly placed security monitors. Linked to the outside world by a state-of-the-art satellite communications facility, the building served as a primary nerve center for the DEA's international war against drugs. There was another security check to go through at the doorway, but the presence of Bonberg eased the process for the three guests and soon they were all in the communications room, where a three-man crew was hard at work keeping on top of the glut of information coming in from field agents around the globe.

Kissinger had asked about the availability of a computer he could use to link up with Stony Man Farm via modem. Bonberg pointed to a corner of the room that was crowded with a system approaching the sophistication of Aaron Kurtzman's setup in Virginia. Although Cowboy had no illusion that he could rival the Bear's prowess with the microprocessor, he'd done his share of programming while working with advanced weapons systems, and it took only a little over ten minutes for him to make the necessary computations and commands to access Kurtzman's computers and have Bear on the other end of a speakerphone.

"Nice bit of work, Cowboy," Kurtzman complimented his erstwhile protégé. "Shows you were paying attention during all those lessons I gave you."

"Damn right," Kissinger said. "Things are starting to break for us down here. I just wondered if you'd had any luck on your end."

"Matter of fact, I've been trying to reach you for the past hour. I've got something pretty disturbing. Sit back and watch your screen."

The others gathered around Kissinger, eyes on the amber monitor linked to the main computer. While the first images were beginning to flicker into view, a phone at one of the other stations rang.

"I got it," Bonberg called out, telling the newcomers, "It's our hot line. Means a big one's about to go down."

As the DEA agent went to pick up the receiver, Kissinger adjusted the screen's contrast, making the data that flashed across the screen easier to read.

"Here's what I started out with," Kurtzman explained over the speakerphone. The left side of the screen had nearly a hundred names separated into three columns, while the other side was crammed with various bits of seemingly disconnected information. "First I listed everyone involved with the expedition, from whatever standpoint—whether they were there or not. Then I started factoring in variables, including any trips over the past six months to New Guinea or drug-producing nations. That whittled the list down to thirteen names."

A transmitting light blinked as Bear touched another button, adjusting the data on both screens to reflect the weeding-out process.

"Then," Kurtzman went on, "I narrowed it down to the past seven weeks. And wouldn't you know..."

Only two names remained on the left window of the monitor.

Juan Jaisez.

Tyne Murray.

"Tyne?" Kissinger muttered. "She's the one who's tagging along with Lyons and company on the second expedition."

"Afraid so," Bear said.

Grimaldi looked at both windows and said, "Doesn't mean she's guilty, though. Could be a coincidence."

"I wish that was the case," Kurtzman said. "But I ran deeper checks on both her and Jaisez. I've got 'em both spending a lot of time in South America at the same time as the purge wars were getting underway. And, what's more, I tracked her through all the data we've got on this Stephen Hokes, and there are just too many coincidences to ignore."

"What are you getting at?" Sergeant Nipwen demanded. "You saying that Murray and Jaisez killed those two guys down in the Keys and then hightailed down to Skyler's Island to lead your people into God knows what?"

"Much as I hate to say it, it seems to add up that way," Kurtzman said. "And I can't raise Able Team by radio down on the island, even though the storm's passed."

"Damn!" Grimaldi slammed a fist into his open palm. "And we came so damn close to getting down here before they left!"

"Brognola's on the phone with Washington. If the CIA people on Skyler's Island are in cahoots with Hokes and Murray, there's really no one down there we can turn to for help," Kurtzman said.

"Well," Kissinger said with conviction, "we're going to get our asses down there, but fast!"

Kissinger hung up his phone at roughly the same time Bonberg was getting off the hot line. Looking over at Nipwen, Kissinger and Grimaldi, he said, "Looks like we've tracked down that shipment of coke from the marina. Rock house down on Aames Street in Liberty City. You guys want to be in on the bust?"

"Depends," Grimaldi said. "While we're out can you have your people line up a plane I can take to Skyler's Island? The sooner the better."

"I'll see what I can do," Bonberg promised.

"That's good enough for us," Kissinger said. "Now let's go crash that party...."

20

For the next hour, the expedition continued upriver without further incident, but the collective mood had been irreversibly changed. Tyne tried to rouse the group from their preoccupation with the shootings they had witnessed, reiterating that on Skyler's Island it was imperative not to upset the local mores. But if anything, her rallying achieved an opposite effect. Schwarz, sitting across from her and Lyons, pretended not to hear, while Lyons listened with increasing agitation, to the point where he finally countered, "Look, Tyne, spare us the when-in-Rome-do-as-the-Romans crap, all right? I don't buy it!" When the woman glanced at him with a look of shock and indignation, he went on, "If we followed that kind of philosophy, half the scumbags we've put out of commission over the years would still be out there plying their trade."

"It's true," Schwarz said, joining in the conversation. "I still can't believe we just froze back there and let some cold-blooded killers get away without a fight."

When Tyne began to defend her position, Sandy interrupted, "Who knows, maybe those were the same people who killed my brother!"

"Hey," Blancanales called back from the lead boat. "Knock it off, all of you! Let's try to get through this one step at a time and save the arguing for later. Hell, you're all making enough racket to spook the koupreys and half the jungle."

"He's right." Tyne looked at the others. "Look, I'm not trying to justify what happened. I just don't think we should lose sight of why we're really here."

"Like the man said," Gadgets repeated, "I think we should knock it off. This isn't helping anything."

Falling into an uneasy silence, the group shifted its attention to the surrounding jungle. Less and less sunlight penetrated the dense overhead foliage, adding further to the sense of gloom and foreboding. Though the Roiyad had fallen back to their rowing with the same measured competence as before, their eyes were no longer filled with the die-hard perseverance and optimism their tribe was noted for. Instead, their gazes spoke of fear and apprehension, and between strokes of their long wooden oars, they began to murmur to one another in low, guarded whispers.

"What are they talking about?" Tyne demanded of the interpreter.

The tribesman looked at Tyne with thinly veiled annoyance. "They're praying for their safety and yours. Do you object?"

Tyne shook her head. "No," she murmured. "Just tell them to keep it to a whisper."

"I already have," the man assured her.

Lyons put a hand on Tyne's shoulder. "C'mon, ease up, would you?"

Tyne jerked away from Lyons, rocking the boat slightly in the process. "Don't you dare talk down to me!" she hissed.

"What's gotten into you?" Lyons said.

"I already told you!" she snapped. "Let's just leave it alone, all right?"

"Fine, fine. Suit yourself." Lyons turned away from the woman and rolled his eyes. Had he really been away from the romance game so long that he couldn't keep a relationship from self-destructing two days out of the starting gate? It sure as hell seemed that way, and he was as angry with himself as Tyne for the way things had soured. He should have known better than to have rushed toward a deeper involvement based on what had essentially been no more than an initial spark of attraction. Overeager, Ironman. That just won't do.

He was still mulling the situation over half an hour later when Blancanales called out, "Whoa! Trouble up ahead!"

The oarsmen, seeing the reason for Pol's cry, suddenly interrupted their smooth strokes and began fiercely backpaddling in an effort to blunt the forward motion of their boats. Fifty yards upriver, a tall, five-foot-thick tree, undermined by erosion of the banks, had toppled across the river, creating an impassable makeshift dam.

"Great," Tyne muttered. "Just what we need."

With consummate effort, the natives were able to veer their craft off toward the eastern embankment well before they would have otherwise collided with the fallen tree.

"Any way to get past it?" Lyons asked, carefully standing in the boat for another look. He could see a few areas where the water was rushing through the thinner limbs of the tree. "Maybe chopping off some of those branches?"

"I don't think so," Schwarz said, taking one of the spare oars and shoving it down into the water to test the river's depth. "Too deep. Anyway, the current's too unsteady to bring a boat up and start chopping."

Tyne scanned the shoreline. "I say we unload everything and portage the boats down the embankment. It should only set us back an hour or so."

"Sounds good to me," Schwarz said.

"Let's do it, then," agreed Sandy.

Tyne instructed their interpreter to pass along the plan to the natives. The man called out to the oarsmen, who listened intently to his every word. Once the two boats were close to the bank, half the tribesmen pushed their oars into the sediment to bring the craft to a halt. One of the men stood up, looking as if he were going to jump ashore and help moor the rear boat. Then, without warning, he suddenly jerked his oar up out of the water and brought it swinging around full force. Lyons was directly in the path of the oar, and although he was able to raise a forearm in front of him to check the blow, he was still hit with so much force that he was knocked from the boat. Another oarsman lashed out at Blancanales, with similar results. The interpreter, meanwhile, took advantage of the confusion to unsheathe his machete and place it against Sandy's throat as he grabbed the woman from behind.

"What's going on?" Schwarz demanded, reaching to his shoulder holster.

"No guns!" the interpreter warned. "Or the woman dies!"

While Lyons and Blancanales treaded water and witnessed the apparent mutiny, Schwarz and Tyne were quickly surrounded by natives, who took away their weapons.

Tyne glared at the interpreter. "Prayers, my ass. You were plotting this with them all along."

"Only since the shootings," the interpreter said. "We know it was slaves that were killed. We won't be next."

In the water Lyons deliberated going for his .45, but gave up that idea when he saw one of the tribesmen snatch up Tyne's Beretta shotgun and level its twin barrels at him. The interpreter told both Able Team warriors to unfasten their shoulder holsters and cast them aside with the guns still in them. It wasn't an easy task to accomplish while treading water, but both men obeyed and watched bleakly as the weapons sank in the deep water.

"And what do you propose to do with us?" Tyne asked the lead native.

"Into the water," he told her and Schwarz. "Now."

"What about her?" Lyons cried out from the water, gesturing at Sandy.

"She comes with us," the interpreter said. "If we get back to our land without trouble, we will let her go. Otherwise she dies."

Sandy stood frozen with fear in the man's grip, feeling a trickle of blood seep down her neck as the machete blade pressed deeper against her flesh. She was afraid to swallow or speak.

"Okay, you win," Schwarz told the interpreter, crouching slightly in the boat, then diving over the side. Tyne followed soon after, leaving only Sandy among the Roiyad.

"How are we supposed to get back?" Lyons asked the interpreter.

"By land," he was told. "You will find a way."

As Tyne and Able Team bobbed in the cold running waters of the Aitacon, the two boats floated away from them, heading back toward the coast, leaving them to whatever fate the jungle might offer.

21

People living in the projects at the edge of Liberty City called it Deadly Aames, a two-block stretch of Aames Street that dead-ended in the same marshland that had proven too unstable for the foundations of eight two-story homes thrown up around the cul-de-sac during a construction boom seven years before. Sagging visibly into the substandard fill, the houses had been condemned and evacuated a year ago, only to fall prey to drug dealers who moved in and made the crumbling shells the site of transactions and a place where buyers could sample their wares and even pass out for the night without having to contend with the fear of recrimination. As their reputation in the underworld had grown, the houses had become a magnet for gangs and other criminal elements, and it was inevitable that the lawless violence marking their daily modus operandi would spill over into the neighboring residential areas. Now it wasn't enough for those in the vicinity merely to steer clear of Deadly Aames; they also had to live in constant fear of burglary, assault and robbery. Murder had even become a sad fact of life in the area, with seldom a week passing without the coroner being called out to tend to yet another victim of the drug wars, be it a willing accomplice in the concentrated crime wave or some innocent bystander who had been in the wrong place at the wrong time and fallen in a drive-by shooting.

Things began inconspicuously enough with the appearance of four semi trucks that rolled to a stop at the edge of the marshland across from the cul-de-sac. The emblems on the sides of the trucks indicated that they belonged to a privately owned landfill firm, and from all appearances it seemed as if some sort of effort was going to be made to beautify what was essentially a barren field that had become an unsightly dumping ground. Fifteen men in hip-high rubber boots hopped out of the trucks and began picking up broken furniture, discarded appliances and other trash strewn across the soggy marshland a few dozen yards away from the old homes; they placed the refuse in giant heaps. Their presence did little to dissuade the regulars making their daily pilgrimage to Aames Street, either on foot or in low-riding cars bearing signature marks of local street gangs. People wandered up walkways of broken concrete and waited on front porches for barricaded doors to be opened just enough for words to be exchanged and cash to trade hands— the first overtures in transactions for cocaine and crack.

All in all, it looked like business as usual.

Then, off on Heath Drive, the street running adjacent to Aames, the engines of five separate bulldozers started up in well-synched unison on the lot of a construction site. Instead of scooping earth or grading slopes, the dozers rumbled out onto Heath and down to the corner. As they turned on Aames and headed for the cul-de-sac, they were joined by a plain-marked but armor-plated Bell helicopter containing a pair of rifle-toting DEA sharpshooters. The chopper began circling high above the condemned houses and an officer next to one of the marksmen bellowed through a bullhorn, "This is the DEA. You're under arrest! Everyone in the houses below, come out with your hands up!"

Down in the marshes, Grimaldi glanced over at Kissinger and Nipwen as he reached inside his hip waders and pulled out his Government Model automatic. "It's show time, boys and girls...."

Kissinger and Nipwen and the dozen other men in the marshes likewise went for their secreted weapons as they began fanning out around the condemned homes. Eighteen more men piled out of the semis, wearing bullet-proof outfits and gas masks. As they stormed past their backup force, they began hurling tear-gas canisters at the closest buildings.

Some of the people inside the homes rushed out immediately, wild-eyed with surprise at having been caught. Others, however, were less willing to surrender, and there was an anticipated crackle of gunfire as unseen dealers lashed out with a variety of illegal weapons, from cheap handguns to automatic rifles.

From their aerial perspective, the chopper snipers were able to draw bead on a couple of gunmen, and a quick volley from their Weatherbys took out both men. One slumped back out of view inside an upper-story bedroom, while the other dropped his M-16 out the window, then followed it, crashing to the ground.

When several dealers tried scrambling to freedom out the back doors of the homes, the backup troops in the marshes quickly pinned them down with warning shots. One gunman tried to push his luck, dashing for his cherry-red '84 Camaro, all the while raking the grounds with 9 mm parabellum slugs from a mini-Uzi.

Grimaldi set his weapon on its deadly three-shot mode and cut the fugitive down five yards shy of the car. Kissinger similarly returned fire at a fleeing gang member trying to cover his flight with blasts from a sawed-off shotgun.

"We sure as hell stirred ourselves a hornet's nest," Nipwen bellowed from his cover behind an old Frigidaire. "We're gonna have to sublet a hotel to keep 'em all on ice!"

The portly officer's wisecrack turned out to be his final words, as he leaned into view just as a rifleman inside the closest house on his right squeezed the trigger. A red gout appeared below Nipwen's eye, snapping his head back with so much force that he was thrown onto his side, where he thrashed for a few fleeting seconds, then lay still in the mud.

"Fuckers!" Grimaldi snarled, dodging from cover and rolling to firing position near a splintered picnic table. He traced the trajectory of the shot that claimed Nipwen and squeezed off four quick blasts, stopping only when he saw an enemy rifleman crumple on the side porch more than forty yards away.

The gas-masked troops, meanwhile, used a small battering ram to crash through one of the houses and vanish inside, spreading out in all directions. There were a few seconds of boisterous gunfire, followed by an even longer period of uneasy silence before the force emerged, dragging nine choking, vision-blurred men with them.

Three of the five bulldozers had moved in on the same house, and when the head of the assault unit signaled an all-clear, the mustard-yellow behemoths groaned toward the building from different directions, each with its steel maws raised up like the claws of mutant crabs in a fifties horror film. As they crashed into the first house, wrenching it from its already flimsy foundation, the walls collapsed in a shower of splinters and broken glass. In a mere eleven seconds, the structure had been flattened to a smoking heap of rubble, debris and packets of drugs that would never make it to the street.

This display of ruthless determination and finality made an impression on most of the fugitives still lurking inside the other buildings. Weapons began flying out into the open and tear-gassed dealers and buyers alike staggered out of hiding, hands raised high as they either begged for mercy or began their cries for a good lawyer.

"Fuck, man," one of them complained as he watched a second house being demolished by the teams of bulldozers. "This ain't right! You trying to kill us all or something?"

"That probably wouldn't be a bad idea," Thad Bonberg said, jerking off his gas mask as he shoved the dealer to the ground and cocked his service revolver against the back of his head. "But for now, just keep your cool while I search for a little something to send you upriver until your kids have gray hair."

Kissinger and Grimaldi backtracked to where Nipwen had fallen. Cowboy checked for a pulse, already knowing he wouldn't find one.

"Tough break, friend," he muttered hoarsely.

"Sure was," Grimaldi said, feeding a fresh clip into his Colt. "But let's make sure he didn't die in vain."

Kissinger nodded. "Yeah. Let's win one for the Nipper...."

As the sweep-up continued, neighbors from the surrounding projects were drawn by the sounds of

gunfire and local police began barricading the streets
to keep them away from the action. Kissinger and
Grimaldi threw themselves back into the thick of
things, trading shots with a handful of diehards
clinging to the absurd hope that they could outlast the
small army assembled to bring them down. It was
Kissinger who put a bullet through a tall, muscular
man attempting to make his getaway with a set of
leather Harley saddlebags filled with coke and crack,
and bearing the same wrappings attributed to the Colombian Mibyche Cartel.

"The guy who did the marina job?" Grimaldi
wondered as he inspected the drugs.

"Could be," Kissinger said. "We saved the taxpay-
ers a few pennies if he is."

"Good, because they'll need the money to pay for
an operation like this," Grimaldi said, waving at the
manpower that had been brought in for the sweep.

The second house toppled to the ground just as
flames were beginning to consume the remains of the
first. Six paramedic vans and four Miami police buses
rolled onto the scene to tend to casualties and would-
be prisoners. In all, three criminals had been killed in
the bust, fifteen had been wounded to various de-
grees, and another forty-five had been taken into cus-
tody. The authorities, in sharp contrast, had suffered
only four casualties, and Nipwen was the lone fatal-
ity.

"Hey!" a voice shouted out amidst all the commotion. "I'm looking for a John Kissinger and Jack
Grimaldi!"

Cowboy waved to get the attention of the man calling his name. It turned out to be Sam Hurst, the pilot
who had flown Able Team to Skyler's Island. Taking

Kissinger and Grimaldi aside, he told them quickly about the circumstances behind the Team's inauspicious landing the night before, then added, "The Corsair's being refueled and should be ready for takeoff any minute. I'm supposed to take you to the airport and fly you back to the island."

"I got my wings, ace," Grimaldi told the man. "You just tell us how to get there and we'll do the rest."

22

His lungs burning for want of fresh oxygen, Lyons swam back up to the river's surface and greedily sucked in the late afternoon air.

"Any luck?" Blancanales called out from the top of the fallen tree. When Lyons shook his head, Pol drew in a deep breath and plunged headlong into the river, taking his turn in the search for the weapons the Roiyad tribesmen had forced them to drop. The Roiyad were now far gone from this spot where they'd abandoned Able Team and Tyne Murray.

Lyons clung to the branches of the tree until his breathing was back to normal, then pulled himself from the water. Tyne reached out to help him up.

"This is a waste of time," she said, still wringing water from her clothes. She stared past him into the brooding waters, where Blancanales was just surfacing empty-handed. "We'll never find those guns and we can't just stay here. The sun's going to be going down soon and we'll be in real trouble unless we find our way to safer ground." She pointed off through the wall of foliage reaching to the east embankment. "Our best bet is to blaze a trail that way and hope we reach one of the plantations before dark."

"And what makes you think we'll get help at the plantations?" Lyons wanted to know. He squeezed water from his light blond hair, then plucked off a finger-size leech that had fastened itself to his forearm, which was already bruised from where he'd deflected the oar blow. As Lyons helped Pol from the water, he asked Tyne, "Who's to say they won't use us for target practice like they did those tribesmen?"

"I just think it's our best chance, that's all."

Schwarz was on the bank, barely within earshot. "I still think we should keep looking for a while," he said as he readied himself to dive. "I don't want to have to take on this jungle with just a stick. Hell, even Tarzan had a knife."

He leapt forward, neatly cutting the surface of the Aitacon and disappearing from view.

"Okay," Lyons finally conceded. "How about if we split up? Two of us stay here and try to get the guns; the others head off."

"Sounds fine to me," Pol said. "I think I'm the best swimmer of the bunch, so it makes sense for me to stay."

"And I know the island and a couple of the plantation owners, so I'll go," Tyne said. Balancing herself on the fallen tree, she crossed to shore and began rummaging for something she could fashion into a club. Lyons followed behind her, exhaling with resignation.

"I'll go with you," he said.

Schwarz surfaced and swam back to shore, where the others told him the plan. He nodded in agreement, telling Lyons, "If you get through to somebody with some transportation, try to intercept the Roiyad first. I'm worried about Sandy."

"I think she'll be okay, amigo," Blancanales said. "She has a good head on her shoulders."

"Besides," Lyons assured Schwarz, "I don't think the Roiyad really want to face the repercussions if something were to happen to her."

Tyne had a watch that doubled as a compass. As she checked it, she said, "It's a little after four. We're going to be heading north by northeast and unless we hit any real obstacles, we'll stick to a straight line so you can try to catch up if you get the guns." She shivered momentarily as a breeze rustled through the jungle against her damp clothes. Snatching up a broken tree limb, she looked at Lyons. "Ready?"

"As ready as I'm going to be," he said.

"Good luck," Blancanales told them.

"You too, homes," Lyons said.

Pol turned back and dove into the river as Schwarz remained on the bank. Tyne set out into the untrampled forest of green, swinging the club in front of her like a machete. She was able to snap back fronds and thinner branches, but it was clear from the onset that progress would be slow. Lyons followed close behind Tyne, using his forearms to ward off the sturdier branches that snapped back at him in her wake. The damp earth sucked at their feet with each step, making grotesque slurping sounds.

"Any time you want to switch places, just say the word," he told her.

"I will," she said. "And thanks for not pulling some macho trip about wanting to lead the way."

"Just trying to mind my manners," he told her. "You know, ladies before gentlemen."

She thrashed through a bed of waist-high ferns, then paused long enough to glance back at Lyons. "Look, about earlier. I'm sorry I flew off the handle. It wasn't called for."

"Apology accepted," Lyons said. "This hasn't been much of a picnic for any of us."

"I know, but I feel somewhat responsible," she said. "I'm the one who lined up the tribesmen, and I'm sure I didn't win any awards for tact the way I badgered that interpreter."

"Well, what's done is done," Lyons said. "Let's just make the best of things from here on in, okay?"

Tyne offered a slight smile. "Fair enough."

They forged ahead, and in another twenty minutes they had traveled beyond hearing distance of the river. Replacing the steady rush and gurgle was the sound of wind rustling leaves in the canopy, as well as the buzzing of insects and the sporadic whistling of birds. Halfway up a sloping knoll, Lyons paused, staring at a large, oblong growth suspended from a low-hanging branch. It was brownish in color and wrinkled, like an oversize prune.

"Termite nest," Tyne told him. "There are tons of them around here. It's one reason there's not too much construction."

Lyons leaned in for a closer look. "Hmm. I always thought in places like this they had ground nests. You know, the tall kind that look a little like volcanoes."

"You're thinking of Africa," she said. "There are nests like that here, but they belong to bleeder ants."

"Bleeder?"

Tyne nodded. "They're red, like fire ants. Also hurt like hell if they get on you."

"Thanks for the warning," Lyons said, reaching into the pants pocket of his khakis for a tube of insect repellent. "I think maybe I better slap on another layer of this before the bugs start looking for supper."

"Speaking of supper," Tyne said, "I wish to hell the Roiyad had had the decency to leave us a few rations. I don't like the idea of having to forage around here for something edible. No matter what you put down, your system's not going to like it and you'll know it by morning."

Lyons didn't reply, and when Tyne looked at him, he had a mischievous grin on his face.

"What's that look for?" she asked.

Lyons hummed nonchalantly as he reached behind him, removing something from his back pocket.

"Come on," Tyne said. "What's this all about?"

"Din-din in a tin-tin," he said, revealing a small tin of sardines. "I kept one of these suckers on hand in case I wanted a snack on the boat."

"Give me that," Tyne said, reaching for the tin.

"Not so fast," Lyons taunted, pulling it away from her.

"Come on," Tyne pleaded. "I already apologized. Don't be a jerk."

"You're going to have to be nicer to me than that," Lyons told her as he backed away. "You might try saying please, too."

"Okay, if you're going to be like that..." Tyne suddenly lashed out with her club, trying to knock the tin from Lyons's hand. He was ready for her, though, and pulled his hand away, laughing as he started jogging uphill away from her. She followed after him, shortening her grip on the club as she called out, "What happened to being a gentleman, Mr. Lyons?"

"What can I say," Lyons told her as he reached the crest. "It's a jungle out there and..."

Looking past Tyne, Lyons's jaw suddenly slackened and he fell silent.

"What is it?" she said, turning around. Then she saw them, too.

Spectacled koupreys. Ten of them, grazing in a field of tall grass more than thirty yards down the other side of the knoll.

"Son-of-a-bitch!" Lyons whispered in awe, recognizing the beasts from pictures Sandy had shown the Team back in Florida. "He was right, after all!"

"I'll be," Tyne muttered, with a little less surprise. She knew that these were probably the same oxen they were supposed to 'discover' near the river. The fact that they were this far inland led her to believe that the men responsible for herding them to the water were still about, lurking somewhere in the jungle, possibly having heard their approach. With the master plan having gone awry, she wasn't sure how to deal with this unexpected finding.

"Shit, and we don't have the camera," Lyons said in frustration. "What should we do?"

"I don't know," she confessed, trying to think fast.

She was spared from having to make a decision when a figure suddenly appeared at the edge of the herd, waving to her and Lyons.

"Buenos dias!"

It was Bernardo Octria, holding an M-1.

"Do you know him?" Lyons asked Tyne.

"No," she lied, waving back. "But let's not look a gift horse in the mouth. If he can help us, I'll be more than glad to humor him. Let's go check it out."

They slowly and quietly started down the slope toward Octria and the koupreys. "I don't get it," Lyons whispered. "A soldier herding oxen that are supposed to be extinct. It doesn't add up."

"Maybe it does," Tyne answered, trying to fabricate a cover story. "Maybe they've just found them and know they're an endangered species."

"I don't know...."

Although he smiled at the rifleman and gave no indication of his uneasiness, Lyons continued to mull over his suspicions. When Tyne offered a salutation in Spanish and the man responded, he closed his eyes, trying to place the dialect. Like the other members of the team, he had such training a few times every month, but he'd never had a real affinity for languages. In this case, however, he already had a preconceived notion, and the more the man talked, the more Lyons was convinced that he was listening to a Colombian.

"We better watch our step," he whispered to Tyne. "I think he's one of the cartel boys."

"No, that doesn't seem likely."

"I'd bet on it," Lyons said, taking a closer look at the man he was waving to. They were less than twenty feet away from each other now. Something about the man's features seemed disturbingly familiar and he finally placed the reason why. "He was in a file of mug shots of cartel people we looked through at the Farm before we set out here."

"You're sure?" she asked.

Lyons nodded, all the while keeping his eyes on Octria's rifle.

"That's too bad," Tyne said as she whipped her club around, catching Lyons squarely behind the head. The Ironman twisted in place from the force of the blow, reflexively battling for his balance. It was a battle he lost, and as a supernova of stars exploded inside his skull, Lyons felt himself falling, falling....

23

During his years as a flyboy, Jack Grimaldi had manned the controls of everything from mower-engine ultralights to supersonic 747s, so for him the Coast Guard Corsair was a piece of cake. Once he reached his desired altitude above the Atlantic, he pushed the small jet for all it was worth, racing against time to reach Skyler's Island.

Beside him, Kissinger gave a quick once-over to the last-minute additions to the arsenal they were taking with them. In his lap was an Armscor grenade launcher, packed with six potent 40 mm HE rounds in a drum cartridge. A loaner from the DEA armory, the launcher represented the ultimate in such weaponry, from its relatively light weight to its multisight capacity. A second Armscor rested in the back of the cockpit.

"Sad to think the DEA needs shit-kickers like this to fight drug dealers," Grimaldi said.

"Sad but true," Kissinger agreed. "You saw the firepower they were using on us back there, and that's tame compared to some of the things I've heard. I tell you, since I left the DEA things have escalated beyond belief. Now you've got dime-bag pushers toting Ingrams and using them the first time someone looks cross-eyed at them."

"Hey, you don't have to tell me," Grimaldi assured him. "I've been there, too. They didn't bring Nipwen down with a peashooter."

"Yeah," Kissinger muttered. They fell silent momentarily, listening to the Corsair's jets as they thought back on the sergeant's self-deprecating humor and his ballsy demeanor at the Shivering Timbers pool table. In his wretched polyester suit, Nipwen hardly looked the part of a hero, but both men knew better. With his passing, the scales had been tipped ever so slightly in favor of the enemy.

"Tough break for the fat man," Grimaldi finally muttered. "He was all right."

Kissinger nodded as he reached for the radio microphone. With great difficulty, he managed to patch into a frequency enabling him to make contact with Stony Man Farm. Hal Brognola had just returned from Washington and was anxious to pass along his findings.

"Jack, Cowboy," he told his two operatives, "we've done full-scale security checks on the Company people operating out of Skyler's and all the other islands of the Caribbean, and they all have some sort of link with Tyne Murray."

"Damn!" Grimaldi cursed.

Brognola went on, "That's not to say that none of our people down there can be trusted, but if our theory about Murray is correct, we really can't take any chances."

Kissinger quickly surmised the bottom line. "So what you're saying is that basically we're going in alone."

"Not completely," the chief said. "I just got off the phone to Bonberg and he's putting together a backup force. They're probably only a half hour behind you, so if you want to slow down or pull a holding pattern over Skyler's Island until they catch up with you . . ."

"Forget it," Grimaldi said. "That black widow Murray isn't going to put her plans on hold on our account, and there's no way we're going to waste time twiddling thumbs when the Team's in danger."

"I had a feeling you'd say that," Brognola said. "And, I must say, it warms my heart to hear it."

"Heart?" Kissinger scoffed. "You have a heart?"

"Easy, lad," Brognola told the weaponsmith. "You're forgetting your commandments."

"Oh, right," Cowboy said. "Thou shalt not think thy boss can take a joke."

"That's not the commandment I was thinking of, actually."

Grimaldi gave his instrument panel a cursory inspection as he asked Brognola, "Have you contacted the government down there? Can't they lend a hand?"

The men in the plane heard a brief burst of bitter laughter on the other end, then Brognola said, "Mayos? Hardly. From all indications we've received, he comes from the Noriega school of drug tolerance. We never found hard proof, but we're pretty sure he did his share of dealing with Panama back then, and we're just as sure he's probably in cahoots with runners in South America. Maybe even the Mibyche Cartel."

"Which means his military probably isn't wearing halos, either," Kissinger guessed.

"That would be my suspicion."

"Well, thanks for all the good news and cheer, Chief," Grimaldi said. "You wanna check and make sure our life insurance is all paid up?"

"You'll do fine down there," Brognola said. "Just be careful."

"Uh-huh," Kissinger deadpanned. "We'll just say whoa."

24

It was on his seventh dive that Schwarz finally felt his fingers closing around the wet leather of a shoulder holster. Exultant, he broke toward the surface with his booty clutched close to his chest.

"Jackpot!" he howled merrily to Blancanales, who was roaming the nearby banks, gathering wood for a fire.

"Madre Dios!" Pol called out when he saw the .45 automatic in the drenched holster. "All right!"

"Of course we're probably going to die of pneumonia from all this diving," Schwarz joked as he swam toward the fallen tree and began to pull himself up. "Man, my skin's so wrinkled I could pass for—"

"Gadgets!" Pol shouted suddenly, pointing toward the other side of the river. "Behind you!"

Schwarz glanced over his shoulder. A little more than a dozen yards away, a fifteen-foot-long black caiman had just crept to the river's edge. Related to the alligator and crocodile, the caiman had distinctive ridges of bone connecting its eye sockets and massive jaws lined with jagged, yellow teeth. With silent ease, the creature slithered into the water, propelling itself toward Schwarz with strokes of its powerful tail.

Schwarz knew at once that he had no time to try pulling the gun from the holster. His only chance was flight, and after flinging the holster up toward the exposed branches of the tree, he clutched for the nearest limb and pulled himself up. Even as he was swinging his legs from the water and wrapping them around the trunk, he heard a sudden thrashing in the river directly below him and heard the snapping of slavering jaws. Refusing to look down, Gadgets swung his weight around, trying to put as much distance as possible between himself and the meat-eater that had apparently added him to the dinner menu. In doing so, however, he put too much strain on the branch and it snapped loose from the trunk, dropping Schwarz back into the river, almost directly onto the caiman.

Spurred on by a jolt of fear-charged adrenaline, Schwarz acted upon what he knew to be his lone chance for survival. Instead of trying to get away from the beast, he now swam toward it, taking care to avoid the deadly tail, which could have easily knocked him out, if not killed him with a well-placed blow. Straddling the reptile's back, Schwarz curled his legs around the long, wide stomach and leaned forward, using both hands and arms to pin the lethal jaws closed. He knew that although gators could clamp their teeth down on prey with mind-boggling pressure, the muscles supporting their jaws were conversely barely sufficient to open the mouth. Schwarz's grip effectively muzzled the beast, and he was riding high enough up on the back to be clear of its tail. Now he only had to hold his breath and hope that his strength would outlast the thrashings of the carnivore, which dropped low in the river as it tried to shake off its rider like some underwater bronco.

Meanwhile, Blancanales abandoned his woodpile and hurriedly scrambled along the fallen tree stretch-

ing across the river. The retrieved holster was fortunately tangled in one of the upper branches, and with
some effort Pol was able to inch close enough to un-
snag it. Removing the .45 from the holster, Blancanales was thankful that it was one of the guns that had
undergone Kissinger's expert retooling, making it fully
waterproof. He had no doubt but that he could fire the
weapon, but as he stared down at the frothing waters
where Schwarz wrestled for his life with the caiman,
he knew that it would be difficult, if not impossible,
to get off a shot without endangering the man he was
trying to save.

Unless... he thought. Dropping feetfirst into the
river, Pol opened his eyes the moment he was underwater and swam toward the mismatched opponents,
gun in hand. Schwarz was still holding on, but it was
clear that both his strength and his lung capacity were
fading fast. There wasn't much time. Pol closed in,
approaching the caiman's underside and pressing the
short barrel of his Government Model against the soft
flesh beneath its jaws.

Schwarz saw Pol's plan and shook his head, then
used his head to gesture at the beast's skull. Blancanales understood immediately and shifted the .45,
pressing it near one of the creature's eye sockets, aiming in toward the small concealed brain. The weapon
was set for 3-round bursts, and when Pol pulled the
trigger, both men leaned away from the beast to avoid
being hit by a stray bullet.

Almost instantly the caiman broke out into a frenzy
of death spasms, writhing with so much force that
both men were thrown clear. They swam off in separate directions. Blancanales grimaced as he felt the
creature's tail strike a glancing blow against his thigh.

It wasn't enough to slow him down, however, and both he and Schwarz surfaced at roughly the same time. It wasn't until they had both dragged their weary frames ashore that they felt safe enough to stop moving, and even then their hearts continued to thump madly inside their chests as they filled their lungs with welcome breaths of air. The caiman churned a few seconds longer, then sank from view beneath the murky waters.

"Thanks," Schwarz told Blancanales between breaths.

"No problem," Pol wheezed. "Just don't get mad that I lost the gun in all the shuffle."

"Aw, gee, I think you oughta go back after it," Schwarz heckled.

"Yeah, right," Pol said. "If I didn't find the gun, I might at least come back with enough gator skin to keep us in shoes the rest of our lives."

"I was thinking more of gatorburgers for dinner," Schwarz confessed.

"Right now I'd be thankful for a good fire." Pol leaned over and began stacking pieces of twig and bark into a burnable formation. "You have dry matches by any chance?"

Schwarz checked his pockets, coming up with a small plastic vial. He carefully unscrewed the top, then tapped out a pair of wooden matches and a small emery board the size of a tie clasp. "Voilà! We're in luck."

As Gadgets was about to strike one of the matches, Blancanales reached out and placed his fingers around the tip. He put the index finger of his other hand to his lips, gesturing for Schwarz to be quiet. Both men listened intently and could finally hear it clearly. Someone was coming toward them down the rough path Tyne and Lyons had made earlier.

"I don't think it's them," Blancanales whispered. "They're trying to be too quiet."

Schwarz nodded in agreement and slowly rose to his haunches. Blancanales did the same and they spread out in opposite directions, disappearing into the dense foliage around them, each carrying one of the larger sticks they'd planned to put in their fire.

Crouched next to a small bush dotted with fragrant orange flowers, Gadgets tried to ignore his chilled bones and the fatigue from his time in the river. Almost twenty years ago, he'd been in a similar position, squatting in another jungle halfway around the world, trying to elude the stealthy approach of the Vietcong. It had been a terrifying experience—and then he'd had an M-16 at his disposal instead of a flimsy stick. But he'd survived, and he vowed to himself that he was going to survive now.

A loud, insistent buzzing suddenly sounded directly behind him, and Schwarz almost betrayed his position by leaping into action against a possible foe. At the last second, however, he saw that the noise was merely that of a hummingbird seeking out nectar from the flowers beside him. He watched the bird with wonder. Hell, if that little thing could beat its wings that fast without tiring, then he could summon enough strength to get through this latest crisis.

Several more minutes passed, then Schwarz saw the first of the intruders. It was a man in khaki, advancing cautiously in a half-crouch, rifle in hand. An old M-1, from the looks of it, Schwarz thought. He'd heard those weapons fired countless times and suspected they had been the source of the gunshots that had felled the two tribesmen downriver and ultimately triggered the mutiny of the Roiyad.

"Thanks for the warning, pal," Gadgets whispered under his breath as he tensed his muscles, waiting for the right moment.

When the Colombian, one of Octria's underlings, wandered to within four feet of him, Schwarz sprang forward, both hands outstretched. One hand went straight for the soldier's throat, strangling the vocal cords and stifling any chance that he could let out a cry of warning. With his other hand, Gadgets gave the man a karate chop to the wrist that made him lose all sensation in his fingers, particularly the one on the trigger of the M-1. The two men fell to the ground under the weight of Schwarz's momentum, and the Able Team commando continued applying pressure to his foe's neck until the man was dead.

Reassured by the feel of a rifle in his hands, Schwarz slowly rose above the foliage, looking down the path, where he saw a second Colombian standing firm, drawing him in his sights. Before the man had a chance to fire, however, he was blindsided by Blancanales. A single, errant shot echoed through the jungle as the two men dropped from view. There were sounds of a struggle, then Blancanales emerged into view, holding the other rifle. Schwarz hurried to join him.

"Colombians," Pol said, looking down at the man he'd killed.

Schwarz nodded, whispering, "Let's see if there are any others bringing up the rear."

Creeping back off into the brush, the men took up positions with unobstructed views of the pathway. "Think they might have gotten to Ironman and Tyne?" Schwarz asked.

"Not sure," Blancanales said. "I only know that at some point we're going to have to head down that path and find out."

"Better sooner than later, don't you think?"

"Yeah."

They waited only a minute before abandoning their positions and starting down the vague trail, unsure as to what lay ahead.

25

Although the north coast of Skyler's Island had weathered the previous night's storm with only modest damage, the gale forces had been extremely destructive elsewhere on the island. And as the final tally began to present itself, Stephen Hokes was in a rage.

The bad news had begun trickling in shortly before dawn. The men at the construction site called to report that the Cartel's luxury trailer had been crushed by a pair of uprooted palms toppled by near-hurricane-force winds that had also bowled over the wrecking crane and much of the framework for the Coastal Sands Hotel. Equally devastating were raging floodwaters that had surged with juggernautlike force across the entire construction site, washing out half-built roads and building plots, as well as sweeping more than twenty tons of stacked lumber out to sea. Five men had been killed when their bunkhouse was flattened, and nearly two dozen other workers had sustained injuries. Eight men were missing and presumed drowned.

"Dammit!" Hokes cursed as he surveyed the ruins of his dream from the distant perspective of his private helicopter. Mickey Boldt, a long-time flying enthusiast, was in the pilot's seat, and he had the chopper under better control than his emotions.

"Dammit is right!" he spat. "Look at that fucking mess! It looks like a disaster area!"

"'Looks like'?" Hokes shouted mockingly. "It *is* a disaster area. We're fucking ruined!"

Boldt brought the chopper down for a closer look. Two men waded in knee-high water across what was supposed to have been the makings of a world-class golf course. Reaching the crumbled remains of a half-built clubhouse, they leaned over and pulled out a body that had been trapped under debris.

"Look at that!" Boldt pointed accusingly. "You were in charge of the construction phase, Hokes! Tell me, how much skim were you taking by using shit materials."

"You don't know what you're talking about!" Hokes countered.

"I don't? The hell I don't!" Boldt jerked his joy-stick, catching Hokes off guard and pitching him against the side of the chopper. "Anything down there that was put up right would have stood up to a tropical storm and you know it!"

"This wasn't just a small storm," Hokes protested. "Hell, it was practically a hurricane."

"Well, maybe we should have taken the time to see just how often these bastards hit, don't you think?"

"I did!" Hokes insisted. "Fifty-four years since there was anything close to this."

"Oh, that's reassuring. It'll probably take us fifty-four years to bail this place out and rebuild."

"Don't blame me for the weather, Boldt." Hokes slammed his fist against the armrest of his chair. "And don't forget that I've got more money tied up in this project than anyone else in the Cartel. I'm losing my shirt on this more than you are, dammit! So get off my case!''

The chopper chased its shadow along the coast as the men wound down from their outbursts and continued to view the shattered remnants of their master plan. Along the four miles they'd thus far traveled, the only thing that had come through the storm unscathed was the airfield. Resting on a slight plateau, it was wet but well above the waterline. Crews were clearing it of litter and debris, including sections of the old hangar, which had lost most of its south wall yet miraculously remained standing. Equally salvageable was the Beechcraft Duke B60 that had brought Juan Jaisez to Skyler's Island. Half the small plane's windows had been shattered and it tilted at an angle where it had been swept off the runway, but there appeared to be no significant structural damage. The pilot was standing by, supervising the men trying to right the plane.

"So what's our plan now?" Boldt finally asked as he touched the chopper down near the old hangar.

"Well, with that expedition going on, I still want to follow through on the getaway plan," Hokes said. "My double will be coming in tomorrow, so I want to get out of here today. Just as well, because I'm going to have to do a little wheeling and dealing to come up with enough cash to get us back on track."

"Back on track?" Boldt said incredulously. "Shit, pal, we're back to square one here."

"I don't know about that," Hokes said. Having calmed down and adjusted to the calamity, he felt there was room for optimism. "I think once the water level's gone down we won't be in as bad a shape as it looks. Now that we have control over more jungle land, we can build back and throw up levees to check floodwaters, and we'll shore things up when we rebuild. It's not the end of the world."

Boldt turned off the chopper's rotors and shook his head. "Sorry, man, but that ain't the way I see it. What's more, I don't like the idea of you skating off and leaving the rest of us to deal with this."

"Don't be an idiot," Hokes told the Texan. "My leaving was planned last night, before we had any idea how bad the storm was. Given what we've seen, it's even more important now that I get to Algiers. There are people there I can get to put up money for a restoration, provided you see to it the press doesn't catch wind of our damages."

Boldt bristled at the tone in Hokes's voice, but he finally managed to rein in his temper. "Okay," he said through his clenched jaw. "We'll play it your way for now and see where it gets us."

"Good," Hokes said. "Don't worry, we'll get out from under this."

The two men climbed down from the chopper and headed over to the grounded Beechcraft. T. W. Glenn glanced over at them, grinning. "Hey, I hope that offer's still on."

"It is if that plane can still fly," Hokes said. He'd called the pilot by radio from the mansion the previous evening, offering him fifteen thousand dollars to fly him to Algiers and back.

"Hey, this baby's in fine shape," T.W. insisted. "Just a few nicks and dents. Gimme an hour, two max, and we'll be ready to fly."

Hokes checked his watch. "Okay, fine."

"What's the story with Jaisez?" T.W. wondered.

"He decided to stick around and enjoy the scenery," Boldt told the pilot.

T.W. laughed as he looked around the wasted coastline. "Must be a sight prettier inland than here, huh?"

"You could say that," Hokes said.

"Oh, that reminds me," the pilot said, turning to Hokes. "You got a call from the plantation. Ed Redsana. Said to make sure you called him back before you left."

Hokes excused himself, leaving Boldt with T.W. and the Beechcraft as he went inside the damaged hangar. Construction workers were reinforcing the weakened corners where the wall had collapsed. The office had survived the night, however, and the shortwave radio was in working order on a desk near the north wall. Despite the fact that the station's transmission tower had been felled by the wind, Hokes was still able to get through to the mansion. Redsana answered.

"I understand the shit really hit the fan down there, Steve."

"The shit and just about everything else," Hokes said. "What's up with you?"

"Well, we have a small problem of our own," Redsana explained. "Our plan with the expedition party didn't really pan out the way we wanted." He went on to relate Tyne's tale of the problem with the natives on the river and their subsequent hiking toward the plantation, which had ended with Lyons recognizing Bernardo Octria.

"What about the other guys in the expedition?" Hokes asked. "Did you get them, too?"

"We've got some guys out looking for them," Redsana reported. "I'm thinking that we ought to question this guy we have; find out how much of our cover's been blown."

"Good idea," Hokes said. "You probably won't get much out of him, but it's worth a try. Look, I'm probably not going to be getting off for another couple of hours. If you get any information I should know about, reach me here, pronto."

"Will do."

Signing off, Hokes began walking out of the office, then paused, seeing someone duck away from the doorway. He calmly reached inside his coat and pulled out a .357 Magnum. Continuing to the doorway, he lunged forward and whipped the gun into firing position.

Whoever had been standing outside the door was nowhere to be seen. The rest of the hangar was dark and empty, save for where the laborers were hard at work on the makeshift supports.

"Hey," he called out to them, slipping the Magnum back inside his coat. "Any of you see someone outside this office while I was on the radio?"

The workers glanced his way and shook their heads. He scanned their faces, looking for the slightest trace of guilt and finding none. Frustrated, he lit a cigarette and headed back outside, just in time to see a Corsair jet descending at a sharp angle from the sky overhead, bound for the same landing strip he and Boldt had used.

"Who the hell's that?" he cried out, feeling a fresh burst of paranoia.

"Beats me," Boldt said.

Hokes took a few steps back, into the shadows of the hangar. "Well, find out and make damn sure they aren't reporters."

"What if they are?" Boldt asked.

Hokes discreetly patted the bulge beneath his coat. "If they are, I'll be in my office."

As Hokes headed back inside the hangar, T.W. looked over at Boldt. "Listen," he said, "if there's gonna be some kinda trouble around here, let me know. I nearly cashed in my chips during that storm last night; I don't feel like pushing my luck anymore."

"Like the man said," Boldt told him, "these are mystery guests. We're gonna have to wait for 'em to sign in before we know if there's gonna be trouble."

"SEEMS TO ME if the Team landed on the other side of the island, we ought to do the same," Kissinger said, peering through the Corsair's windshield as Grimaldi brought the jet down.

"You heard the boss," Grimaldi said. "He didn't want us riling the militia if it could be helped."

"True, but look at this place. You think anyone here's really going to give a shit about some expedition, much less know what route they might have taken?"

Grimaldi shrugged. "What can I say? If we strike out here, hopefully we can score a car and find a road to the city that hasn't been washed away."

Enough debris had been cleared from the landing strip to allow the Corsair to touch down and roll gracefully to a stop close by the Beechcraft and helicopter. Grimaldi killed the engines as Kissinger set the grenade launchers in the back cabin. "We can come back for these later," he said. "These folks outside look a trifle antsy, so we shouldn't make them any more nervous than necessary."

"Agreed," Grimaldi said.

As they got out of the Corsair and climbed down to the ground, Kissinger and Grimaldi were met by T. W. Glenn and Mickey Boldt.

"'Lo," Boldt greeted the men. "You folks having plane problems or something?"

Grimaldi shook his head. "We tried reaching you on our radio but there was no answer."

"Equipment's a little flaky since the storm," T.W. said.

Boldt scratched his chin and said, "Reason I asked is that, as you can see, we aren't exactly in a position to offer much in the way of accommodations. Where you guys from, anyway?"

"Mainland," Grimaldi answered. "We have some friends down here on an expedition. We want to make sure they didn't get rained out."

T.W. frowned. "You're a little late, fellas. I remember hearing about an expedition, but that was a good week, week and a half ago. Had some problems, too, I think."

"I don't think that's the one they're talking about," Boldt told Glenn. Eyeing Kissinger and Grimaldi, he asked, "Who's with that group?"

"Tyne Murray," Kissinger said. "She's part of the consortium here."

Boldt nodded. "That's right. I know Tyne. Real nice lady."

"Then you know if they managed to head out today?" Kissinger asked.

"I'm not sure about that, but we can check." The Texan gestured toward the hangar. "C'mon inside. T.W., keep cracking on that plane, okay?"

Glenn shrugged and went back to rejoin the workers laboring around the Beechcraft. They'd managed to right the plane and were inspecting the wings. One of the men pointed out something to the pilot, who whistled, shaking his head. "Yo!" he called out to Boldt. "Got ourselves a wing crack here. Gonna have to put those takeoff plans on hold."

"We'll manage somehow, I think," Boldt said, casting a surreptitious glance at the Coast Guard Corsair. Reaching the hangar entrance, the Texan turned to Kissinger and Grimaldi. "Can you wait here just a second while I check with the boss?"

"No problem," Grimaldi said.

As soon as Boldt passed through the doorway, closing the door behind him, Kissinger and Grimaldi looked at one another. Cowboy spoke first, in a whisper.

"That guy has about as much finesse as a fart at a funeral. He's got foul play written all over him."

Grimaldi raised an eyebrow. "Trap?"

Kissinger nodded, reaching inside his coat. "I'd bet the Farm on it."

"I won't tell Brognola you said that," Grimaldi said as he went for his automatic, too.

The men were standing out of view of the men repairing the Beechcraft. They drew their guns and took up positions on either side of the doorway. Kissinger checked the doorknob. It wasn't locked. On a count of three, he threw the door open and both men charged in.

Their suspicions were well-founded. Boldt was just in the process of telling Hokes they could kill two birds with one stone by taking care of Kissinger and Grimaldi and using their plane for the flight to Algiers. Hokes never got a chance to reply. When he saw the two gunmen bursting into the corridor outside the office, he immediately bolted from his seat, drawing his Magnum.

"Freeze!" Kissinger shouted.

Boldt obeyed the command, throwing his hands upright and glaring over his shoulder at the intruders. Hokes, however, seemed to be in a good position to make his getaway out through the gap in the wall until his way was blocked by the sudden appearance of one of the construction workers. Before Hokes could react, the worker had let lose with a roundhouse punch, striking him squarely on the jaw. Hokes fired a wild shot to the floor as he staggered back into a file cabinet, clinging to the barest thread of consciousness. Several of the other workers, alerted by the gunshot, poured through the wall to see what had happened.

"I lost some good friends last night," the worker shouted at Hokes and Boldt with uncontrolled rage as he rubbed his bruised knuckles. "And all you care about is covering your asses and trying to cut your losses. Well, guess again!"

The man grabbed Hokes's fallen Magnum and looked ready to use it on him when Grimaldi cautioned, "Don't!"

"He deserves to die!"

"Probably," Grimaldi conceded. "But not here; not now."

The worker hesitated a moment, then slowly lowered the Magnum. He leaned forward and spat at Hokes. "Scum!"

Grimaldi frisked Boldt and came up with a small Colt Cobra, which he slipped into his pocket. Kissinger circled around the desk and loomed over the fallen man in front of the file cabinet.

"Stephen Hokes, I presume."

T. W. Glenn and the men who had been working on the Beechcraft rushed into the office, two of them carrying wrenches as if they were battle-axes. The sight of Kissinger and Grimaldi with 1911-A automatics dampened their heroic fantasies, however, and they dropped the tools to the floor.

"We're clean, man!" T.W. explained frantically, directing his pleas to Grimaldi. "Hey, I'm just a dumb flyboy-for-hire."

Grimaldi flashed his special-agent badge for the benefit of those in the room, and as he and Kissinger tied up their two prisoners, they asked for the probable whereabouts of the expedition team. Neither Hokes nor Boldt was volunteering any information aside from a mantric chant about their rights and their demand to have an attorney brought to their side.

"We're working on it," Kissinger said, "but it's not like we can just have you pop a dime in the pay phone, y'know?"

"But tell you what," Grimaldi said, sorting through Boldt's keys and finding the one that worked the helicopter. "We'll go looking for one, okay?"

"You won't get away with this!" Boldt threatened.

"Hey, you're stepping on our lines," Grimaldi chortled. He went over to the man who had helped prevent Hokes from escaping. "You up to being deputized?"

"Uh, yeah," the man said. "Sure."

"Good." Grimaldi placed Boldt's Cobra into the man's hand, then pointed to Hokes and Boldt. "Make sure they stay put. If they don't, kill 'em."

The man with the gun smiled for the first time that day. "Gladly."

Leaving the hangar, Kissinger and Grimaldi strode to the waiting helicopter. Cowboy looked over his shoulder at the wall of jungle rising up to his right. "Lotta island out there, Grimaldi. We could run out of fuel a dozen times and still not be close to finding them."

"You got any better ideas?" Grimaldi asked.

Kissinger shook his head and climbed in the passenger's side of the chopper. Grimaldi took the pilot's seat and quickly familiarized himself with the controls as he warmed up the rotors. Satisfied, he maneuvered the throttle and joystick, bringing the copter aloft.

"I guess we'll just hit the interior and start circling back," Grimaldi said. "I figure we have an hour of daylight left, tops, so cross—"

"Jack! Over there!"

Grimaldi looked and saw that Kissinger was pointing off at the far edge of the airfield, where a solitary figure was walking purposefully across the tarmac. As they drew closer, the figure looked up and began to wave.

"I'll be damned," Kissinger muttered with disbelief. "It's Sandy!"

26

The first thing Lyons saw when he regained consciousness was a man-size anthill, rising up into the air six feet away from him, framed by the green background of the jungle. The sun was just settling behind the treetops, and when a ray poked through he closed his eyes and grimaced, turning away from the glare, aware of a firebrand of pain burning away at the back of his skull. At almost the same moment he realized that he could move neither his arms nor legs. He was on his back, limbs tied to stakes pounded into the ground.

What the hell was going on? he wondered.

He thought back, searching for answers. His skull continued to throb, making it difficult to concentrate. Finally he began to recall certain incidents. The jungle. Koupreys. A Columbian. Rifle.

Tyne.

The puzzle fell into place—at least in terms of how he'd blacked out. The other question still nagged at him, however.

What the hell was going on?

"Ah, finally awake, are we?" It was a man, behind him. New England accent. Lyons craned his neck but couldn't see his questioner. He could, however, see another figure on the ground next to him. It had once been human, but now there were only skeletal bones covered with flies.

"He looks a little...undernourished, wouldn't you say?" Ed Redsana said as he walked into view and grinned down at Lyons.

"You," Lyons whispered hoarsely, recognizing the man who had supplied the ill-fated expedition.

"Yes, that's right." Redsana crouched beside his prisoner, picking up a closed jar of honey that had been lying on Lyons's stomach. He unscrewed the lid and dipped his finger in, then sampled the contents. "Mmm. Nice and sweet. Would you like some?"

"Go to hell," Lyons told the man.

"What's that?" Redsana said. "Yes, you want some? Well, since you ask so nicely..."

The bearded man tipped the jar slightly, letting honey drip down on Lyons's chest, just over the heart. "Oh, clumsy me."

Lyons ignored his pain and tried to look around, asking, "Where's Tyne?"

"Over there," Redsana said, pointing off in the distance. "She's waiting by the car. You know women...a few ants and they get all squeamish."

Just out of the corner of his eye Lyons could see Tyne leaning against the side of a jeep. She was watching him, unmoved and unmoving. "Hurry up, Ed," she called out impatiently. "Don't take all day with this."

Redsana sighed. "Very well. Tell us, Mr. Lyons. How much do your people know about our lit-tle...operation?"

"Go to hell," Lyons repeated.

"Certainly you have a wider vocabulary than that."

"Go to hell."

"Mr. Lyons, this just won't do. I'm offering you a reasonable—"

"Go to hell."

"Suit yourself." Redsana shrugged and began pouring a thin trail of honey from Lyons's chest down to the ground and over toward the myriad swarm of ant nests. "I doubted you'd have the sense to save yourself."

Redsana was about to set aside the honey when a shot suddenly rang out. He shouted with pain as the jar shattered in his hand. Dumbfounded, he reached for his revolver and looked around, trying to see where the shot had come from.

"Over here, fuzzface," Blancanales said as he stepped out into the clearing and swung his M-1 rifle into sharpshooter position. "Come on," he taunted. "My trigger finger has an itch. Scratch it."

The ant nests lay between the two men, and Redsana ducked quickly to one side, thinking they would provide adequate cover. Blancanales, however, merely shifted the rifle to one side and fired twice. Both shots ripped easily through the nests, losing little velocity en route to their intended target. Redsana groaned as the bullets bit into him, spinning him off balance so that he crashed headlong into one of the nests, drawing further ire from its six-legged tenants. Within seconds, tens of thousands of ants had streamed onto him, bringing forth the same pathetic, helpless screams that Juan Jaisez had imparted the day before.

Schwarz, meanwhile, emerged from another section of the forest and bee-lined for Lyons. More of the ants, drawn by the scent and taste of spilled honey, were pouring down from the nearest nest and inching their way toward the bound commando. When he reached Lyons, Gadgets crouched over the first of the stakes and tugged at it, pulling with all his weight. As the ants charged closer, Blancanales reached his Able Team comrade and clawed at another of the posts.

"Hurry, dammit!" Pol seethed, feeling ants creeping up the inside of his pant legs and through the thick hairs on his calves. He willed himself to ignore them and continued helping Schwarz try to free Lyons.

Overhead, the harsh drone of a chopper announced the arrival of Kissinger and Grimaldi, who had brought Sandy with them. The rotor wash of the craft's whirring blades bent the grass of the clearing and further agitated the nests.

During the commotion, Tyne saw her chance for freedom and circled around to the driver's seat of the jeep. It was only then that she realized, to her horror, that the keys were with Redsana, who was in no position to give them to her. Ducking low so as to avoid detection, she began feverishly tugging at the ignition connections, hoping to hot-wire the car.

Lyons felt the razorlike pincers of the ants going after the honey covering his shirt, and as soon as he had one hand free he beat on his chest, then ripped at the buttons, sitting up and yanking the cloth from his body. Blancanales and Schwarz finally pulled up the pegs binding his ankles, then reeled away from the nests, swatting at their own bodies, trying to rid themselves of the voracious insects.

Rising to his feet, Lyons fought to retain his balance and stared at the chopper descending twenty yards away from him. The sight of Sandy with Kissinger and Grimaldi raised his spirits immensely, but his euphoria was quickly checked when he saw Tyne, at the far edge of the clearing, starting up the jeep's engine and shifting gears into reverse.

"Noooo!" he bellowed, charging across the grass. Tyne backed up and turned the jeep around, flooring the accelerator. In his weakened state, Lyons knew he had no chance of catching up with her. Glancing to his side, however, he saw Kissinger bounding out of the chopper with one of the Armscor grenade launchers and held his hand out, shouting, "Let me have that!"

"What for?"

"Just give it to me!" Lyons snapped, wresting the weapon from Kissinger's hands. Dropping to one knee, Lyons propped the launcher against his shoulder and placed one eye up to the sights.

"I owe you, lady," he said as he pulled the trigger, "and I always pay my debts."

The Armscor bucked sharply into Lyons's shoulder, but he paid no attention to the blow. His attention was on the retreating jeep, which was about to disappear into the jungle when the 40 mm HE charge struck. The resulting explosion drowned out even the thunderous sound of the rotors, and a cloud of smoke obscured the fate of the obliterated target.

Leaving behind his gaping partners, Lyons strode determinedly toward the jeep, which had been flung from the dirt road by the force of the grenade. Split and twisted, the vehicle now lay on its side, and one wheel continued to spin eerily, though the engine had stalled. Tyne had been thrown clear and was lying in an unnatural position at the bottom of a small ditch, one arm twisted behind her back and her lifeless eyes staring up at the distant treetops.

Lyons stood at the upper edge of the ditch watching her, his expression blank. A few stray ants continued to crawl over his bare chest and he absently swatted them away.

"Okay, Ironman," Kissinger said, coming up behind Lyons and laying a hand on his shoulder. "Let's go."

Lyons stayed put a moment, then slowly turned and headed back with Kissinger toward the clearing, where the others awaited him. Up in the nearby trees, he could hear the chatter of monkeys. "They're laughing at us, Cowboy," he said grimly. "And we deserve it."

EPILOGUE

When Gardner Richwell arrived on Skyler's Island three days later, the floodwaters had receded from the south coast, exposing more rubble and debris from the ravaged construction site. All the bodies of fallen workers had been recovered and flown back to the States for burial. Those men who remained behind did so with the understanding that their paychecks for the next few weeks would be coming from the government, with Prime Minister Mayos's signature and blessing for their part in helping to remove any reminder of the Coastal Sands debacle. With the disbanding of the Cartel, Mayos was seizing control over the coastland with the promise of returning it to its former untrampled state. For now, at any rate, Skyler's Island was out of the running for tourist dollars and, at least until the heat died down, Mayos and Timeli weren't likely to be pursuing plans of cocaine cultivation or Communist collusion.

Landing on the runway in his private plane, Richwell first noticed the makeshift holding pen that had been erected next to the damaged hangar. Inside the pen were twenty-one spectacled koupreys, awaiting the arrival of a cargo ship that would transport them to Miami and the Metrozoo.

Sandy Meisner was waiting by the corral when Richwell deplaned and walked over. Gadgets Schwarz was with her.

"This must be a proud moment for you, eh?" Richwell told Sandy as he watched the oxen mingle near the feed troughs. "Your brother's legacy is assured, thanks to you."

"Not just me," Sandy said, winking at Schwarz. "I had plenty of help."

"Of course," Richwell said, offering Schwarz a handshake. "Good job. That's quite an outfit you belong to."

"The best," Gadgets said. He looked over at the hangar, where Lyons, Blancanales, Kissinger and Grimaldi were helping T. W. Glenn put his Beechcraft Duke B60 back in running order. Although only Grimaldi had any appreciable experience working on planes, the others had easily picked up the rudiments and moved about with assured precision, lending an efficient team effort to the proceedings.

"Yeah," Schwarz repeated, "they're the best."

Nile Barrabas's most daring mission is about to begin . . .

THE BARRABAS BLITZ

JACK HILD

An explosive situation is turned over to a crack commando squad led by Nile Barrabas when a fanatical organization jeopardizes the NATO alliance by fueling public unrest and implicating the United States and Russia in a series of chemical spills.

Phoenix Force—bonded in secrecy to avenge the acts of terrorists everywhere.

Super Phoenix Force #2

American "killer" mercenaries are involved in a KGB plot to overthrow the government of a South Pacific island. The American President, anxious to preserve his country's image and not disturb the precarious position of the island nation's government, sends in the experts—Phoenix Force—to prevent a coup.

Out of the ruins of civilization emerges...

DEATHLANDS

The Deathlands saga—edge-of-the-seat adventure not to be missed!

			Quantity
PILGRIMAGE TO HELL became a harrowing journey high in the mountains.	$3.95		☐
RED HOLOCAUST brought the survivors to the freakish wasteland in Alaska.	$2.95		☐
NEUTRON SOLSTICE followed the group through the reeking swampland that was once the Mississippi Basin.	$2.95		☐
CRATER LAKE introduces the survivors to a crazed world more terrifying than their own.	$2.95		☐
HOMEWARD BOUND brings the journey full circle when Ryan Cawdor meets the remnants of his own family—brutal murderers.	$3.50		☐
PONY SOLDIERS introduces the survivors to a specter from the past—General Custer.	$3.95		☐

Total Amount	$	
Plus 75¢ Postage		.75
Payment enclosed		

Please send a check or money order payable to Gold Eagle Books.

In the U.S.A.	In Canada
Gold Eagle Books	Gold Eagle Books
901 Fuhrmann Blvd.	P.O. Box 609
Box 1325	Fort Erie, Ontario
Buffalo, NY 14269-1325	L2A 5X3

GOLD EAGLE®

DL-A

Please Print
Name: _____

Address: _____

City: _____

State/Prov.: _____

Zip/Postal Code: _____